Charm City Spouse's Club

by

Pamela Kyel

Charm City Mystery Series

The Wild Rose Press, Inc.
PO Box 708
Adams Basin, NY 14410-0708
Visit us at www.thewildrosepress.com

Publishing History
First Edition, 2025
Trade Paperback ISBN 978-1-5092-6001-0
Digital ISBN 978-1-5092-6002-7

Charm City Mystery Series
Published in the United States of America

Dedication

To the lights of my life.
Melina and Natania.
My babies. My girls.
May your tea be as sweet as you are
and your lives like your cups—full to overflowing.
I love you.
I believe in you.
Always.

Chapter One

"That is one fine man, right there," Cassy said.

"Who?" I craned my neck to see where she was looking.

"Third baseman. What's his name?"

"I don't know him—he's Army. Besides, don't you already have a tall, dark, and handsome man in your clubhouse?" When she turned toward me, the confusion was evident on her face. "Hello—Amaré?"

She let out her great guffaw of a laugh, and the people in front of us turned around, but we didn't care.

"Naw, man, Amaré and me just friends. We're just friends."

"Why?" I asked.

"Whatchu mean, why?" she asked. "I don't see him that way, and he definitely don't see me that way."

"I think he does see you that way, and you don't see it," I said.

"Naw, man, it ain't like that," Cassy said.

I chose not to argue with her because today was about softball and sunshine—sweet tea and even sweeter friends. It meant taking some much-needed time with my two favorite people, yelling at the umps when they got a call wrong, and cheering on my co-workers.

This was the friendly rivalry game held every summer between the Air Force Office of Special

Investigation (OSI) and the Army Criminal Investigation Division (CID) based at Aberdeen Proving Ground. It was my first time attending since I moved back to Maryland this past winter.

As Special Agent Laci Duvall for Air Force OSI it was my job to solve cases involving members of the military. Many times, we also assisted the local police in their investigations. Speaking of local police, I swiveled my head back and forth, looking for Baltimore Police Detective (BPD) Antonio Desio. We recently reconnected after twenty-plus years, and I was waiting for him to ask me out again. Our first attempt failed after we wrapped up my ex-husband's murder a month or so ago, and he may have given up on me when that fell through.

"You see Antonio anywhere?" I asked.

Cassy Davis was one of my roommates and also a former BPD officer. Sammie Wheaton was my other roommate. She and I recently met while investigating the murder of my ex-husband and her current one, Special Agent Zach Wheaton, AFOSI. It's a long story—but you already read that one, right?

"Nuh-unh," Cassy said.

"Well, don't that beat all?" Sammie was back from the bathroom with her and Zach's twins in tow. When she reached us, she sent a "mom" look behind her to the crowd. It didn't bode well for whatever upset her.

"Wha's wrong?" Cassy asked.

"There's only one working stall in the ladies' restroom, and the person in the working one is taking their own sweet time. I gave up and took the twins into the men's room. I swanny the men act like they've never seen a woman in their bathroom before."

Ana climbed up to me, and I leaned my elbows back on the seat behind me so she could settle on my lap. Ryan clung to Sammie while she maneuvered the bleachers to take her spot on my other side.

It was a gorgeous day in Edgewood. It was the halfway point between Aberdeen and our office in Golden Ring. The fields sat next to a new center called Edgewood Neighbor Space, but it was a separate entity. Some major calisthenics were performed to get this, which raised our collective blood pressures in more ways than one.

Colonel Waters served as the OSI coach. He took it pretty seriously and voiced his disappointment in me for sitting this one out. I couldn't even pretend to play softball. I tried in high school, but my coaches wrote me off as hopeless when I kept getting hit by the balls instead of catching them. This meant I was assigned to right field, where I admired Desio playing baseball on the field behind us.

"So, wha's happening with you and Desio?" Cassy asked.

"You know as much as I do," I said.

"He ask you out, yet?" Cassy asked.

"Not since our failed attempt last month," I said. "I'm waiting to see if he tries again."

Cassy tipped her head back and laughed, and Sammie leaned around me to see what she was laughing about.

"You gonna be waitin' forever if it's up to him—so instead you gotta ask. Whatchu think, Sammie?"

"You think it's okay for the girl to ask out the guy?" Sammie asked.

"Sure. Why not? This here the twenty-first century.

3

I seen the videos on social media where the girl asks the guy out all the time. Don' bother them any—why should it bother you? I betchu he asks you out before the week is up, though."

It was my turn to tip my head back and laugh. "Yeah, like that'll happen."

"How much you wanna bet? Fifty?"

I whistled. "That's steep. But then I could stand to take your money."

We shook on it, and Cassy hopped up from her seat. "I'mma try and use the can."

I took the opportunity to stand, and swung myself and Ana off the bleachers. I was placing her on the seat in front of me when the whistle blew for the middle of the third inning. Ana quickly covered her ears with her hands, and I placed mine over hers. It was what I'd seen Sammie do for her another time.

The Army came in for their turn at bat, and our newest OSI member jogged out to shortstop. Captain Wesley Hanscom knew one end of the softball bat from the other, and it showed. She wasn't afraid to get dirty and frequently dove and jumped her way into catching the uncatchable balls hit by the Army. Which is why it was strange when she suddenly missed a practice throw less than an arm's length from her right side.

She stood staring at something behind me, and I turned and immediately brought my fist back to release it on someone dumb enough to sneak up on me. Antonio caught it with agility, just like he did the last time I took a swing at him.

"Oh, good," I said, "it's you."

He grinned with my fist secured in his hand. "You hungry?" he asked.

"I could use some sweet tea," I said. "Sammie, you or the twins need anything?"

"Nah, y'all go on," she said.

I made sure Ana was secure and joined Antonio to go to the concession stand. I was debating whether to ask him out when a scream went through the mingling crowd around us. A quick scan in front of me showed everyone was looking toward the women's bathroom. So, without thinking anything about it, I took off for the crowd with Desio a step behind me.

We forced ourselves through the people, and I could see Cassy over the head of everyone. I covered my ears a split second before she whistled through her fingers to get everyone to pipe down.

"There ain' nothin' for you to see here," Cassy said. "Go on."

If only the people listened to her. Instead, Desio and I resorted to throwing elbows and dodging phones after she jerked her head for us to continue to the front. This didn't bode well for the softball game going on behind me. When we finally reached her, she opened the door with one hand while she held the arm of a woman in a polo shirt with the Neighbor Space logo in the other. The woman looked like she'd just seen a ghost. *Oh, just hell.*

Desio and I squeezed through, and I saw her before the door slammed shut behind me. Instead of joining them in the stall, I about-faced, grabbed the door handle, and flung myself outside. Fighting through the crowd again, I honestly didn't care who I pushed out of the way. I landed on my hands and knees twenty yards from the front door. With nothing but water in my gut, that's all that came out—cups and cups of it.

After I unloaded, I waded back into the fray. When I reached the door, I covered my eyes with my left hand and pushed the bathroom door open with my right. Someone was talking with Desio and Cassy.

"They called me to te—you okay, hon?" I assumed she was talking to me, so I nodded and told her to continue. No way was my hand coming down before it was ready. "They called me to tell me that one of the bathroom stall doors was locked from the inside. Since there isn't enough space for someone to crawl through or climb over we have to have someone with a key come in and open the door, you know? Lucky me, that was my job today."

"Do you know this woman?" Cassy asked.

"No idea. I'm not new here, but then I'm not one of the ones who've been here the longest, you know? Kinda in between. I see all sorts of people in and out of here, so I can't say if I have or haven't. I could have, but my mind for faces isn't what it used to be. You know?"

"Were you the one that found her?" Cassy asked.

"Sorry about the scream. It's not every day you encounter a situation like this in my line of work."

"What did you touch in the room?" I asked.

The woman addressed my question. "Just the outside door coming in and, of course, the doorknob here."

"Cassy, would you mind taking Ms…" Desio began. We waited for the woman to supply her name, but it took her a second. A beep sounded to my right, and one glance showed Desio hanging up his phone and putting it back in his pocket.

"Oh." She jumped. "I'm Doris McCain."

"Cassy, would you take Ms. McCain and get her information for us?" Desio asked.

"Sure." Cassy reached for her elbow again, but she was already at the door.

"I swear, I've never seen anything like this before in my life. You know?" Ms. McCain said before the door shut her outside.

"You ready to do this?" Desio asked.

I nodded and dropped the hand covering my eyes when he pushed open the stall door with a paper towel over his finger. In front of us, propped up against the stall wall, was a woman in her late thirties or early forties. Her blonde hair was up in a ponytail, and her bangs stopped at her eyebrows. She wore a yellow polo shirt with little daisies on it and white shorts. She had sand and dirt on her legs, which ended with white shoes and white socks sporting yellow pom poms on the back. The scene was unremarkable except for the plastic pink flamingo with metal stakes for legs protruding from her chest. The blood must have run under her shirt because there was hardly any to be seen on her front. Her hands were crossed in her lap as if she were just sitting at a picnic.

Desio reached for the pulse, and she fell forward into his arms.

"Shit," he muttered.

I stared at him in shock but then quickly tried to help him with the body. The area was small, and there was only so much I could do. He went to lay her on her back on the concrete floor, but then I saw the legs of the flamingo came out the other side—along with the pool of blood. It appeared the blood took the metal legs as a guide and dripped down the stakes onto the toilet and floor behind her.

"Wait, the stakes—" I said.

He knew what I meant, and we slid her on her side and propped her against the portion connecting the two stalls.

"You called this in yet?" I covered a sulfur burp with my fist and turned so I could see none of her.

"It's outside my jurisdiction, so I could only call the Harford County Sheriff. They should be here in a minute or two. They're right down the road."

Cassy pushed the door open behind me. "You guys, I got somebody out here who wants to talk whichu."

Desio joined Cassy outside while I stayed with the woman—I looked everywhere but at her. I tried looking for clues, but my eyes strayed back to her. She looked at peace—as crazy as that sounds. Thankfully, he was only gone a matter of minutes before he returned with someone else. She wore almost the same outfit as the dead woman but with different patterns and colors.

"Major, this is Candice Landis. She said her friend Jill was missing after going to the bathroom about an hour ago."

Candice stopped in shock. Her mouth hung open, and nothing came out, but suddenly, her face met the floor. Desio and I were caught by surprise, which is why neither of us caught her in time. We watched in horror as her head bounced on the rubber mat covering the ground by the sink.

Desio reached under her arms and hoisted her to a stumbling position. We were almost to the door when it opened for us, and Colonel Waters stepped inside but stopped short when he saw us.

"What in the wild blue yonder is going on in here, Major?" he demanded. "Oh, sweet Moses."

"Excuse us, sir," I said.

Desio escorted Candice Landis to a group waiting by their cars in the parking lot. A few tried to ask him questions, but he walked away from them. The door closed before I saw where he went.

"Do you know her, sir?" I pointed to the woman in the awkward position on the floor in the stall.

"Yes, that's Jill Westfall. Her husband is Major Noah Westfall. He's in the Contracting Command at Aberdeen. She was recently elected to the spouse's club as their president. My wife knows her but wasn't friends with her—more like acquaintances. My wife's best friend was running for president also but lost."

"Who is the base commander at APG, sir?"

"General Sandy Fields," he said. "She's tough as nails but is fair in all her dealings."

"Do you know her personally, sir?"

"Just by reputation. But it looks like I'll be meeting her soon enough." He wiped his hand down his face, and the door opened behind me. Desio came in and reached out to shake Colonel Waters's hand. "Hello, Detective Desio."

"Is the sheriff here yet?" I asked.

"Yes, they just got here. They're questioning Candice and other members of some club?"

"The local military spouse's club. How many of them are there, sir?"

"It's different from year to year," Colonel Waters said. "Since the post is small, the number of members is small. So, maybe twenty to thirty?"

"Is there video showing the—" I broke off when

the door opened behind me. A man in a sheriff's uniform stepped in, and we all looked at each other in silence. Then I stuck my hand out and introduced myself. "Special Agent Laci Duvall, Air Force OSI." He looked at my hand like it held the plague before reluctantly meeting it. He released me two seconds before we finished shaking. I raised my eyebrows and looked at Desio while Colonel Waters introduced himself.

"Why is the military here?" he asked. I still didn't know his name.

When Colonel Waters didn't speak, I volunteered the information. "Because the members of the softball teams are Army and Air Force members."

This man was a stale sweet tea in a bottle that'd been lost in the back of the fridge. He didn't even spare me a second glance, just kept his eyes on Colonel Waters, while my statement hung in the air.

"I don't believe you introduced yourself, sir," Colonel Waters said.

"Deputy Robinson," he barked. "Now, I need you to clear out of here so my men can get to work."

"Actually, since this is family of an active-duty Army officer, we won't be going anywhere," I said. Let's see how he liked that.

"This is out of your jurisdiction," he said. Surprised the hell out of me that he acknowledged me.

"No, it's not," I said.

He closed his mouth, and his face turned red. It almost matched the shirt under my crossed arms. One glance at Colonel Waters and I knew he was following along despite how he appeared. The same went for Desio.

You could see the sudden change take over Deputy Robinson. His scowl went away, and his face cleared, but the shifty eyes remained. Before he could speak, the door opened again behind him.

"Y'all ready for me?" A man, no more than five feet even, stepped inside. "You must be the special agents everybody's whisperin' about out yonder." He indicated "yonder" with a chin jut to the door. "I'm Dale Earnhardt, and no, I'm not the racer. My mom and daddy were just big fans of Dale Senior. I'm an Assistant Medical Examiner working for Harford County and several others. You ready, Felix?"

Dale was all southern sweet tea, and I liked him immediately. The same could not be said for Deputy Felix Robinson, who looked ready to blow.

"Hi." I reached my hand to Dale to shake his. "I'm Special Agent Major Laci Duvall. This is Detective Antonio Desio with the Baltimore Police Department, and this is my boss, Colonel Jack Waters, also AFOSI."

"BPD? Why are you here?" Deputy Robinson asked.

"He's here because he's with me," I said. "We were observers up until about thirty minutes ago." Robinson didn't like that, but he would have to deal with it. Desio wasn't one to stick his nose in where it didn't belong, but I knew if I needed his help, he would provide it. "Well, we'll get out of here, Doctor Earnhardt, and let you get to work."

"Y'all can call me Dale or Doc, but just don't call me late to dinner." He laughed. Yep, I liked him already.

"Thank you, Dale. Here's my card. You can give me a call and let me know what you discover. Call anytime; this is a priority for me."

Once we were outside, Desio, Waters, and I gathered together for a small meeting. We were immediately joined by the perky shortstop, Captain Wesley Hanscom. She introduced herself to Desio and probably would have kept her hand in his if he hadn't dropped it like it was hot.

"Major, I'm going to leave you in charge here. I need to meet my wife and see what she can tell me. Keep me informed."

"Yes, sir. I'll look forward to hearing what she has to say."

"Me too," he grumbled before walking away.

I turned back to Desio, who stood in uncomfortable silence, perfectly aware that he was under scrutiny.

"Can you excuse us, Captain?" I asked. "We have things to discuss."

"Oh, I don't mind. You can discuss them in front of me if you like. Looks like I'm going to be assisting you anyway." She didn't address me at all but spoke right to Desio.

"Well, I do mind," I said. "No one has indicated you'll be assisting me. So, until that time comes, you don't need to be here."

She finally sensed my tone and turned toward me. I was shocked by the transformation which took place in the blink of an eye. All the sunshine and roses from a second ago were gone and in their place was ice. If looks could kill, I would be dead.

"Whatever you say, *Major*." Then she walked away. I knew right then and there I would have my hands full with her.

"I don't think she likes me very much," I said.

Desio shrugged and flipped open his notebook.

"You don' think who likes you very much?" Cassy and Sammie joined us just then, with the twins hanging off Sammie's hands. When Ana spotted me, she ran over, and I scooped her up in my arms and settled her in her place of honor on my hip.

"My new co-worker," I thumbed over my shoulder to where she stood with several other softball players. "She replaced Major Roberts. Her name is Captain Wesley Hanscom."

"Wesley. Now ain' that a man's name?"

"Nah, I reckin' I knew at least three Wesleys back in Tennessee, and one was a girl." Sammie played a game of peek-a-boo with Ryan behind Cassy while she spoke to us. "Course, I knew a man named Kim, too. Just goes to show you how versatile names are."

"Why don' she like you?"

"It's just a hunch, but based on the amount of time she looked at me versus how much she looked at Desio here, I'd say there's quite a chance he's the reason."

Cassy tipped her head back and laughed, and Desio looked confused.

"Why is that funny?" I asked.

"How much longer we gotta be here?" Cassy ignored my question and asked one of her own.

"What do you think, Desio?" I asked.

"There's no need for me to stay since this won't be my job."

"Oh, you're going to help," I said. "Just think of it in terms of consultation and research."

Chapter Two

My suspicions about Hanscom were confirmed when I stepped into our building the next morning. I didn't even get to set my bag on my desk before Colonel Waters called me into his office.

"Yes, sir?" I asked.

"Sit down, Major, please. Have you been updated on the spouse's club case?" When I shook my head, he went on. "According to my wife and the spouse's club grapevine, the number one suspect they have so far is a fellow club member. Her name is Ruby Moffat. Her husband, Damian, and the husband of the deceased woman are co-workers. Not only that, but they are neighbors and currently deployed together. While Jill's husband, Noah, has been recalled, Ruby's hasn't."

"Have they called Ruby in for questioning, sir?" He wiped his hand down his face and placed his head in his hands propped up on the desk. I never saw him like this before, not even on our deployment a few years ago. "Are you okay, sir?"

"My wife's best friend is Ruby Moffat," he said.

All of a sudden it hit me like a ton of bricks what he was trying to say, and I collapsed in the chair behind me. It looked like I would have to work with Hanscom after all. *Damnit*.

"So, that means you're stepping away from the investigation," I said. He nodded but didn't say anything. "I'm working with Hanscom on this or is there someone else?" *Please, God*, let there be someone else.

"Is something amiss, Major?" he asked.

"I'm not sure. It's more of a feeling right now, sir."

He continued to stare at me but didn't say anything. The knock on the door interrupted our conversation before it got any further. I was relieved until I saw who it was.

"Enter," Colonel Waters barked. I may have jumped a little at the command.

"Good morning, sir." Hanscom beamed as she threw the door open. She was so enthusiastic with her entrance the door bounced off the filing cabinet behind the door. Then she saw me, and her face fell—trust me, the feeling was mutual. It was plain she didn't want to work with me any more than I did her.

"Good morning, Captain, please come in. We have much to discuss."

Hanscom was dressed in OCPs, just like the rest of us. I finally got a good look at her when she stepped forward and turned away from me to sit in the other chair in front of Colonel Waters. I noticed the buttons on the back and realized she was wearing a maternity uniform.

Once she sat, she finally met my gaze, and the ice was the same as yesterday. Funny, I didn't notice anything indicating she was pregnant when I saw her at the softball game. Should she really be diving for all those balls if she was expecting? I side-eyed her profile. No evident bump yet. I mentally shrugged and turned my attention to Colonel Waters.

"Captain, I know you haven't been with us long,

15

but your record of previous cases assures me you know what you're doing. I asked you in here to inform you both I will not be heading this investigation since my wife is best friends with the accused."

"Does that mean the case is all mine?" Hanscom asked. She jumped upright and almost fell out of her chair.

"No, Captain. The case will be headed by Major Duvall here. You will assist her *if* she needs it." So, he had sensed my reluctance to work with her.

Hanscom swiveled her head to me and narrowed her eyes like an owl who had cornered their soft, fluffy prey. "Oh, that will be wonderful, sir. I'm sure I can be of help to *Major* Duvall."

I don't know why she said my rank like she did, but it didn't bode well for our relationship.

"You can discuss the preliminaries now if you like, Major Duvall, or you can request a time later when you're all caught up. I've emailed you the information I have and officially signed off on the case. I would say keep me informed, but I need to be kept out of it completely. I don't want my wife asking me questions and then having to withhold information from her. If I'm completely in the dark, then I can be honest with her about my ignorance of the ordeal. Understood?"

"Yes, sir," Hanscom and I said at the same time.

I stood and Hanscom was a beat behind me. I grabbed my bag off the floor and exited his office. I would need to catch up on emails before I could devote my attention to the case.

When I reached my office, I turned to close the door behind me, but Hanscom stood there. She watched me with an intensity I could admire if only it wasn't directed at me.

"Yes, Captain?"

"Will we be discussing things now?" she asked.

"I'm not going to discuss anything before I've read what Colonel Waters sent me. I'll let you know *if* I need your help." She didn't say anything. "When are you due, Captain?"

She looked confused for a minute before bringing her hands up to her stomach. Still no visible bump.

"Not for a while yet," she said.

"Are you and your husband excited?"

"I'm not married."

While maintaining eye contact, she took a step back into the hallway and did a pretty good about-face on one heel before disappearing from my view. I closed my door behind her and breathed a sigh of relief. I didn't usually have a problem with co-workers. That was until my last one tried to kill me—I've been a little wary ever since.

Despite being in the building for half an hour already, my computer wasn't booted up. Now, with my CAC card in the computer, I leaned back in my chair while it signed me in. The birds were on the feeder outside the window—I noticed they were getting low on seed. I needed to run to the store later and grab some. It was unspoken that it was my job to keep them happy and fed. I was the one who installed the feeders once I weeded out the courtyard and the collection of junk that once called it home. The office was happier with the clutter gone, and we got to see and hear nature. A win-win for everybody.

I located the email from Colonel Waters. Thankfully, it was only sent to me. Waters really meant

I could do this on my own if I wanted.

About halfway through the document, my phone rang in my bag under the desk.

"Major Duvall," I answered.

"Good morning, Major. This is Dale. From the park yesterday?"

"Good morning, Dale. What can I do for you?"

"I just wanted to touch base with y'all before I sent the email over with my report."

"Oh, wow, you're fast," I said.

"Yes, ma'am, I do try. The metal stakes that serve as the legs to the flamingo punctured her heart, but that's not what killed her. A 9mm bullet rattling around inside of her did the job. I found it as soon as I released her fluids. It came right out with—are you okay?"

My head was buried in the trashcan, and I was dry-heaving. See, I didn't even have to be present with the body; the description alone was enough to set me off.

"Yes." I coughed. "I'm fine. Can we skip to the end?"

"Whoever killed her really wanted her dead," he said.

"Any fingerprints?" I asked.

"I have a few partials, but nothing conclusive. Nothing rang in the system either. In a situation like this, prints aren't going to help much, though."

I knew this, but I wanted to check anyway.

"What did the entry point look like?" I asked.

"Entry was clear. I don't reckon she was shot in the bathroom; I mean, she could have been, but then—that ain't my specialty. I know they make things now that keep death clean and quiet."

"Is all this in the written report, Dale?"

"Yes, ma'am. I'll send it right over."

We hung up, and no sooner did I have my cursor in position to open Dale's email than my phone rang again. It was Antonio.

"Good morning, Antonio. To what do I owe this honor?"

I could hear muffling and rubbing on the phone on the other end, but no Desio. I looked at my phone then said his name a few more times, but when nothing happened, I hung up. Two minutes later, he called again.

"What?" I said.

"Laci?" he asked.

"Yes, Antonio, it's still me. Did you need something?" There was some more shuffling, and at one point I think he dropped the phone. "Antonio, are you okay?"

"Doyouwanttogotodinnerwithmetomorrownight?" he gushed.

I stared at my phone in shock. "What?" I asked.

"You're seriously going to make me say that again?"

A hysterical laugh bubbled up and escaped before I could stop it. "Are you nervous, Antonio?"

"Laci—answer the damn question."

I clapped a hand over my mouth after my laughter escaped. He *was* nervous. He was also adorable. If someone carrying a gun could be called that.

"Yes, Antonio. I would like to go to dinner with you tomorrow night."

His heavy exhale carried across the line, and I felt the pressure release all the way to my toes.

We agreed he would pick me up at six and go to

Sapore Di Mare over in Joppatowne. It was a local Italian place with out-of-this-world pizza and pasta. Yes, we could have gone to his parents' restaurant, but it was too far of a drive for the middle of the week.

Once I hung up with Antonio, I switched back into work mode and scanned the report from Dale. There wasn't anything there he hadn't told me over the phone. I wondered if there were any cameras tuned in to that portion of the park. Hmmm, Neighbor Space next door might have something I could check. I would see if anything was propped up on the outside of the building that might be pointed in the general direction of the ballfield.

Next, I returned to Colonel Waters's email and finished reading it. His wife, Kristen, was concerned for her best friend Ruby. The campaign for president of the spouse's club was rigorous and included everything from debates to polygraph tests. The latter was a result of some of the accusations Jill hurled at Ruby. Ruby passed with flying colors, but that didn't keep Jill from accusing her of tricking the test.

The other officers of the club were VP Candice Landis whom I met yesterday in the bathroom. I never saw her once I escaped, though. Candice's husband served in Public Affairs. They were both in their thirties. The secretary was Haylee Bishop—hadn't met her yet. She and her husband were in their late twenties. The treasurer was Miles Manson. His wife was in charge of Military Personnel—hadn't met him either. They're in their early forties. Quite the spectrum of ages in the officers.

During the softball game, the spouse's club's booth sat mixed in with a few other tents like Public Affairs,

Retirement Services Office, and the Suicide Prevention Program. There were five or six tents providing information or services. The spouses were apparently selling cookbooks.

Why would Jill resort to lying about Ruby? What did the lies consist of? The polite thing to do would be to contact Deputy Robinson to see what he found, but I nixed the idea and went back to Colonel Waters's office.

I waited outside his door for the command to enter after I knocked on the door. I hadn't seen him leave, so I assumed he was still here. Just when I was ready to give up, the door opened and Hanscom appeared. She didn't stop when she saw me but barreled through while making her escape.

"Come in, Major," Colonel Waters said. "What can I do for you?"

I gathered he didn't want to discuss what happened with Hanscom, but I could guess what it was about. After one last glance at the slamming farther down the hallway, I entered his office and shut the door behind me.

"Sir, do you think it would be okay to speak to Mrs. Waters concerning the spouse's club? I'd like to get insider information on the vibe of the group as a whole. I'd also like to hear more about the lies that were spread by each of the potential presidents."

"I anticipated you'd like to speak to her, and she has agreed to see you. She wants to clear her friend's name as quickly as possible. She's convinced Ruby had nothing to do with it."

"What about you, sir? Do you think she had nothing to do with it?"

"Captain's quarters, Major, I can't even remember what she looks like, let alone whether she could murder someone or not."

I bit back a grin at his exclamation. "Thank you, sir. Do I need to call her and set something up?"

"Yes, yes—here's her number." Colonel Waters handed me one of his business cards, and I flipped it over and found his wife's name and number on the back. "She's expecting to hear from you today."

"Thank you, sir. I'll call her right away."

"Uh, Major, do you think you will be needing the help of Captain Hanscom for this investigation?"

I slowly pivoted from the office door, dropping my hand from the knob as I turned. There it was. She had whined to the boss.

"I really can't say, sir. Is it necessary that I have her assistance?"

"No, no, Major; it's not necessary. She's chomping at the bit to get a *good case*."

"Sir, we all have to put in our time with cases that aren't 'good.' " I used the air quotes on him. "She just got here. Yes, her record could be great from other assignments, but she hasn't yet shown what she's worth here. Frankly, it's concerning to me that she's so adamant about this particular one. She's still a captain, and that means she takes a backseat to those of us with more experience. She'll get her turn."

"Yes, yes, you're right, Major. Forget I asked." He waved me off with his hand, and when I pulled open the door, Hanscom stumbled into the room.

"Can I help you, Hanscom?" I asked. "Where's your glass?"

I stepped around her as she mumbled excuses as to

why she fell into the room when I opened the door. I mean, everyone knew if you were going to listen at closed doors, you needed a glass to help funnel the sound. They taught us that on day one in OSI school.

Chapter Three

Mrs. Waters agreed to meet me at the coffee shop close to Golden Ring Mall the next morning. It was the same one where I'd met Anne Carson the day before she died. I didn't want to go back there, but it was what Mrs. Waters asked for.

With only a picture of her from Colonel Waters's social media profile to go on, I scanned the small shop hoping she stood out. For about two minutes, I paced back and forth squinting at my phone then at the patrons in the coffee shop—when suddenly someone spoke to me from behind.

It wasn't my fault, really—I swear, but if the woman was any taller, I would have sucker punched her in the chest. Since she was shorter than I was and stood back a little, my fist glanced off her arm and knocked her purse off her shoulder.

"Oh, my God, I'm so sorry! Are you okay?" I was mortified and brought the offending fist up to my mouth and bit it as hard as I could.

"You know, Jack warned me about sneaking up on you, and I did it anyway, didn't I?" She must have realized I was confused because she stuck her hand out for me to shake it. "I'm Kristen Waters."

"Oh, noooo." My horror tripled—I just hit my boss's wife. I covered my face with my hands and groaned, but instead of berating me, she let out a girlish giggle. She was adorable.

"Oh, hon, it's okay. I can count myself among the lucky ones who lived to tell the tale." She laughed again.

I finally set my hand in hers for a handshake after leaving her hanging. She motioned to the front of the coffee shop, and we went and got in line. We placed our orders and waited in silence for ours to be ready—it was definitely an awkward wait. Her hot tea with cinnamon took no time, while my decaf peppermint mocha took a bit longer. What? I liked Christmas in August—didn't everybody?

Once we were seated, she looked at me expectantly. She wasn't at all what I would have thought Colonel Waters would choose in a wife. She had light-blue eyes, and her nose held freckles. She pulled her readers out to look at the credit card display when she paid but took them off, and her eyes were clear and focused. She was petite in height and wore pink shorts with a white leopard print T-shirt—on her feet were slip-on boat shoes. She was cute.

"Did you have some questions for me?" she asked when she noticed I had yet to say anything.

"I'm sorry for staring," I said. "It's just I've known Colonel Waters for so long, and this is the first time I've met you, and you're not anything like I expected."

She tinkled her laugh again, and I noticed her cheeks took on a pink tinge. *Shit*, did I embarrass her?

"Jack is a little bit older than I am. I say a little bit but he's six years older than me. I'm not quite fifty while he reached it a few years ago."

"Oh," I said, "you must be around my age then. I'm forty-three."

"I have a few more years on you, but yes, I'm closer to your age than I am his."

"Wow. How did you meet?" I leaned my chin on my fist with my elbow resting on the table. I knew none of their story.

"He came home on leave one July, and I was home for summer break from my freshman year of college. My family lived next door to his. We hadn't seen each other in years, but suddenly, it was like we saw each other for the first time in our lives instead of what it actually was—us growing up together.

"I was there for his first date with my older sister and then again when she broke up with him for her now husband. We have pictures of our families together on holidays and vacations. There are a few prom pictures of him and my sister, too."

"Wow," I said. This was a whole other side to Colonel Waters. We sat there in silence again until I jerked myself to the present. "Oh. Yes. The investigation. What can you tell me about the deceased?"

"I didn't know Jill outside of the club. Being Air Force and her Army, there really was no socializing. What I observed was inside the club. She was very by the book and rules oriented. When it came to running her campaign, though, nothing was off-limits. She threw everything she had at the operation and didn't hold anything back."

"What were some of the things she did?"

"She had no scruples when it came to winning. She would do what she could to come out on top. She's the polar opposite of her husband, Noah, who is very laidback. He was passed over for his below the zone promotion this year, and it didn't even faze him. He just shrugged and got back to work—he's a very hard worker. He realized he'd get it when he was in the zone, and it didn't bother him.

"Jill, however, took it personally. She thought Noah should have gotten the promotion below the zone instead of Ruby's husband, Damian. She forgot the biggest distinction between them, though. Damian is a West Point graduate, and that makes all the difference in the world to the Army. It shouldn't, but it does."

I nodded—didn't I know that. I lost out on many cases because I didn't have the fortitude to graduate from the Academy. Maybe I should remind Hanscom of that.

"What were the lies Jill spread about Ruby?" I asked.

"I don't intend to spread gossip, but I realize some information is important to figure out who did this. In light of that, I'm relating information which can be substantiated. When I said Jill would do anything to win, I meant it. She told some of the spouse's club members that Ruby slept with her husband's boss, and that's how he got promoted. Colonel Chandler is no longer stationed here, so it was an easy lie to spread and one not so easy to disprove."

"Where did he go? Didn't anyone try and find out if this was the truth or not?"

"Most of the women in the club are there for social gatherings and thrive on gossip. It made no difference to them or not if it was the truth.

"Ruby was also accused of creating a divide in the members. When Jill joined, she immediately went on the offensive and established opposing camps among the members. She didn't like the old president and did what she could to undermine her word and create division in the club. Jill's followers soon regarded the old president and her friends as the enemy. Suddenly her name was dirt to half the club when she never did anything to them—all because Jill took an immediate dislike to her.

"This was before I joined the spouse's club, so I only have Ruby's word for it and a few others who are still around."

"Where is the former president now?" I asked.

"Her husband retired, and they moved back to Wisconsin to run their family's farm."

"How long ago did Jill become president? It sounds like this wasn't her first time running for the position."

"This was her second time running but her first time campaigning against someone. Poor Ruby didn't stand a chance. When Jill got the power that came with the position, God forbid anyone get in her way."

"I don't understand. What kind of power comes with the position?" I asked.

"Generally, the sponsors to the club are the spouses of the post commanders. Everyone wants to be their best friend. Before Jack came to a remote location, we were on a base in California. Never again will I do that. Women lined up to be the base commander's wife's workout buddy despite never having stepped foot in a gym in their lives. I vowed then and there I would never do that.

"Having the ear of the commander's spouse is intoxicating and can go to your head. I've met many who didn't let it get to their heads, but I've also met those who do. Jill was one who did."

My phone ringing in my purse derailed my train of thought just then, and I quickly reached in to grab it. Seeing it was Antonio and thinking he had news on the case, I asked Mrs. Waters if I could take this before I ducked outside to answer it.

"Yes?" I asked.

"Laci? I'm sorry, but I'm going to have to give you a raincheck on dinner tonight."

"What?" I demanded.

"Something's come up, and I can't make it."

I sucked in a breath and let it out through my nose. I made sure he could hear it. "Fine, Desio. I have to go—I'm in the middle of something."

It figured he would do this to me. Not only had I already paid Cassy fifty dollars for losing the bet, but now I would never get it back from her. I hauled open the door and stepped inside the air-conditioned café while I rubbed my stomach. This did nothing to ease the knot of disappointment in my gut.

"Is everything okay?" Mrs. Waters asked.

"It's a wonder there are any children in this world when men do stupid things," I said.

She looked at me in surprise and then grinned. "Problems with Detective Desio?"

It was my turn to look surprised. I didn't know why I was when I told Colonel Waters as much as I did. "Yes, we finally had a date scheduled, and then he goes and bails on me." My phone rang again, and seeing who it was, I dropped it back in my purse without answering.

"Did he say why?" she asked.

"I didn't give him the chance to," I grumbled. "I

don't need to hear excuses."

"How d—" She stopped when I glared at her.

"I know you're trying to help, but I don't want it right now. I want to be mad. I've been waiting for him to ask for weeks, and now that he finally has, he goes and cancels on me in less than twenty-four hours, *and* I've lost fifty bucks in the meantime."

It was clear I'd lost her on that last bit.

"What? Fifty dollars? Why? Wait—why did you wait for him? Why didn't you ask first?"

"You know you're the second person to suggest I do the asking in the last few days," I said. "I don't know. Maybe I'm just old fashioned and think the guy should do the asking."

"Are you sure that's why?" she asked.

"Well, there's the chance he could say no. I walked away from him over twenty years ago, and what if he's still mad? What if this is all a scheme to get back at me for leaving him? Why am I telling you this? I just met you."

She waved that away.

"From what I've heard about him, I don't think he's one to hold a grudge. Jack spoke highly of him and said he could see the sparks flying off the two of you. Sometimes, it's easier to tell someone who doesn't have direct knowledge of either of you."

I felt my cheeks turn warm at that. I didn't know why I got so mad at him over what was probably an innocent reason for calling off the date. I would call him back the minute we wrapped things up here.

"Do you have anything else about the case you think would be important?" I asked.

"I really can't think of anything right now, but I'll

let you know if I do."

"Would you be able to set up a meeting with me and Ruby? And maybe the rest of the spouse's club's officers? I think it would be helpful to hear from them."

"I can do that." She nodded. "I'll get back to you when I have it set up."

We said our goodbyes, and I sat in my car with the air conditioning running a bit before I dialed Antonio's number. He picked up on the third ring.

"Desio," he said. "No, stop that." He spoke to someone in the background.

"Desio?" I asked.

"Laci," he said. "This is—no—"

"*Major* Duvall? What a coincidence. I was just talking to Antonio about you."

I stared at my phone—stunned. Why was Hanscom with Desio? "I'm sorry you were just talking to *who* about me? Forget that. *Why* are you meeting with Detective Desio?"

"Because it's my job. Hello. You're not the only one who investigates for the OSI—but I'm not finished." I couldn't hear what Desio said to her, but suddenly he was back on the phone.

"Laci, I don't know why she's here. I haven't been able to get through to Colonel Waters. Talk to him and get back to me." He hung up.

What the hell was going on here? I dialed up Colonel Waters right away.

"What?" he said. He answered this way when he was distracted—which was a lot.

"Colonel Waters?" I asked. "Can you tell me why Captain Hanscom is with Detective Desio?"

"Megaphones and muffins, Major. I didn't know

that's what she was about when she informed me she was off to speak to someone about a case she's working. I would never have let her go if I'd known."

"That's what I figured, sir. So help me when I see her again…"

"Major, not to be a fly in your ointment, but have you considered the term, keep your friends close but your enemies closer?"

"No, sir, and I'm not about to start now."

****

I screeched to a halt in my parking spot out front of my townhouse, but it did little to get rid of the tension in my shoulders. I didn't agree with Colonel Waters that I needed to work with Hanscom. She was proving my point in every way, too.

Slamming the door shut behind me after I stepped inside did nothing to erase the knot in my gut either, but I did it anyway. Cassy leaned her head back on the couch and stared at me down the hallway outside the kitchen.

"You home early to get ready for your date?" She couldn't keep the Cheshire grin off her face.

"No." I slammed my bag down on the table by the front door. "Turns out there is no date." My purse fell off the table, so I reached down and grabbed it. "Desio called me while I was in an interview and canceled on me." I slammed my bag down again. Harder this time. It fell off again and again I reached down and grabbed it. "Not only that, but when I called him back, he was in the presence of one Captain Wesley Hanscom."

I slammed it down on the table a third time, and when it fell off this time, I punted it down the hallway. My phone flew out of the bag and missed Cassy by inches. The other contents disappeared to parts unknown, but I didn't care.

"Well, hell," Cassy said. "You wanna go to the gun range and get rid of some of that frustration?"

"Who's frustrated?" I asked. "I'm fine."

"Yeah, you look fine."

"Where's Sammie?" I asked.

"Her car died while she was getting the kids from daycare, and her dad went and got her. He'll drop her off here when they done. Sure you don' wanna go shoot stuff?"

"You know what? Suddenly, I'm in the mood to blow through some targets. What's say we name each one?"

"Tha's my girl."

Chapter Four

Cassy drove her car and the bass drew the attention of everyone along the I-695 and 795 corridors. When we pulled through the gate to the gun range and found our spot, the stares continued. Normally, I hated the attention, but tonight I was itching for confrontation. So, instead of shying away from the eyes of others—I met each and every one. Not once was I the first to turn away.

After we checked in, we got our targets and set up the table in our lane. We hadn't been here since we tried to teach Sammie how to shoot a gun last month. I put on my head gear and checked my guns. Cassy was ready to go, so I let her go first. She nailed every one dead center.

"Who was on your target?" I asked her when she finished.

"Desio," she said.

"Really? Why?"

"Because he pissed you off. Ain' no one messin' with my bestie. Even if he is your honey."

"Oh, he's not my honey." I took my turn and unloaded without pulling my finger from the trigger. The tightness in my chest started easing.

"Hunh, you really is mad ain' you?" Cassy said.

"You have no idea."

When Cassy got in position, my phone rang.

Looking at the screen I saw it was Desio. Cassy started firing, and I answered.

"What?" I asked.

"Laci? Where the hell are you? I can barely hear you."

"You know you sure cuss a lot more than you did a month ago."

"It's you," he said. "You bring it out of me. Now, where the hell are you?"

"I don't have to tell you that," I said. "You canceled on me so I can do whatever the fu—hell I want." I pressed end on my phone.

"Who that?" Cassy asked.

"Who do you think?"

"Desio?" she asked. I nodded. "Man got a lotta nerve, I tell you what. Why he cancel on you anyway?"

"He didn't tell me," I said.

"So, it coulda been work?" she asked.

"Yeah, but that's not the point," I said. "The point is it took him this long to ask in the first place."

"You two both so scared of what the other one's gonna do—you lucky you get anything done. He at least gotta reason to be scared."

"Now what the hell does that mean?" I asked.

"You dumped him once. How you know he ain' scared you gonna do it again?"

"Because I've told him I wouldn't do it again," I said.

"Just like you told him twenty years ago you'd always be there?"

"Shut up and shoot, Cassy."

"Uh-hunh. You know I'm right. It ain' my turn—it's yours."

I knew she was, but it didn't make it any easier. I stood and took my place and pushed out all thoughts of our fight, but in its place came the memory of him holding me when I was here the last time. When the darkness took over for a brief second and I was back in the sandbox, being hit from all sides by al Qaeda.

"I'm scared too, Cassy." I turned toward her without firing anything. "What if he hasn't forgiven me? What if I ask and he says no?"

She came and stood in front of me. I looked up, and her face showed only concern. "You one of the bravest, most kick-ass women I know. You can do this. You can' live not knowing. It eats you up inside. If he says no, then you move on, but I don't think he'll say no."

I expelled the breath I was holding, picked up my gun, and took my place in front of the target. When I pulled the trigger this time, the target was my fear and doubts. If only I could annihilate them as easily as I could the target.

****

We were almost to our exit when Cassy's car stuttered to a stop on the side of the road. She banged on the dash above the steering wheel, but it didn't do any good.

I called Sammie while Cassy got out and stared under the hood. We were still a good twenty minutes from home, so walking wasn't an option.

"Hey, Laci, are y'all home?" Sammie asked.

"No, we're stuck on the side of I-695. Are you home? Can you come get us?"

"I wish I could, but Daddy just left to see if he could do anything with my car. Dangit."

"It's okay. I figured it was worth a shot." Cassy opened the door and got in. "Sammie's a no-go."

"Yeah, well, so is the car. I don' know what's wrong with it."

"Can you call Amaré to come get us?"

"He workin' tonight. What about Desio?"

"If he canceled our date, what are the chances he's going to be free to come get us now?"

"True dat."

"We'll have to call a ride-sharing company." I pulled up the map on my phone to find the closest one. "Looks like the closest is called Revved." I dialed him up, and he answered on the first ring.

"What?" he asked.

I pulled my phone back and looked at the screen. I wasn't expecting that kind of reaction. "Is this Revved, the ride-sharing service?" I asked.

"Yeah, you need a ride?"

"Uhhh, yes?"

"Okay. Where you at?" he asked.

I rattled off our whereabouts and included the mile marker we passed a little way back, then hung up.

"He said he'll be here in a few," I said.

We left the car up on the shoulder and retreated about twenty yards into the woods that bordered the interstate. Every once in a while, a semi would drive by and the dirt, sand, and miscellaneous items would kick back on us.

A glance at my phone told me it was twenty minutes after nine when a small, scuffed blue hatchback pulled up behind us. I crossed the barrier on the roadside and approached the driver's window. His shoulder jerked as he manually rolled the window down.

"Hiya, hon. Are you Laci?" he asked.

"You must be Revved," I said.

"Yep, that's me. You guys ready to go? The Os are in the middle of the eighth, and I don't want to miss the ending."

I felt a gurgle of laughter come up and turned wild eyes to Cassy, who joined me on the side of I-695.

"This him?" Cassy asked.

He must have been feeling gentlemanly because he rolled out of his car, and wow, he was enormous. Cassy was no slouch at six foot in flats, but this man stood head and shoulders above her. It hurt my neck to look at him. He was a tall, cold-brewed drink of iced tea—no sugar needed.

"How the hell you fit in that car, man?" Cassy asked.

"Custom seat," he deadpanned. "This all of you?"

We nodded, and he opened the door behind him, and Cassy dove in the back. I guess that meant I was up front.

"I'm Steve, by the way, but you can call me Rev. Everybody else does." He put his hand out for me to shake once we were belted up and ready to go.

"How come Rev?" I asked.

"I'm an exhausted preacher who left the church five years ago. They couldn't pay me enough to stay. So, now I do whatever the hell I want, and what I want is to meet new people on a daily basis."

"Wow," I said. Little did I know how the phrase "Do whatever the hell I want" could take on such new meaning. The man drove like a bat out of hell. Literally. He swerved, he honked, he tailgated, he yelled, but above all else, he swore like a drunk sailor home on leave. I was astonished with the words he strung together and how creative he was with them.

I took a chance at one point and turned around to where Cassy sat wide-eyed and white-knuckled in the back seat. A drive, which under normal circumstances should have taken twenty to twenty-five minutes, Rev did in ten. No kidding. At one point, I think his speedometer broke because it couldn't register that high.

It wasn't just his accelerating that was fast. His stopping was too, and I had honest-to-God whiplash by the time we reached my house. He pulled into the spot out front of my house and hit the brakes so hard, Cassy's head bounced off the back of my seat.

"Holy shit," Cassy said.

"What?" Rev asked. He honestly didn't know.

"That was… Thank you for the ride, Rev," I said.

"Here's my card." He handed me a business card after I signed for the drive, and scrawled on the back was his personal cell number. "Call me anytime, hon." He winked. "I'm local."

I choked on a laugh, opened the door, and got out. He peeled out of the spot and probably left marks on the blacktop. Then he pulled in front of someone on Philadelphia Road, accompanied by the telltale sign of a horn honking.

"Wow," Cassy said. "I can say I ain' never had a car ride like that before in my life."

"Well, he got us here in no time. Your neck okay?"

"Hunh? Yeah, it's fine."

It was nine thirty when we walked through the front door. I expected Sammie to be home, but she was nowhere to be found.

"Looks like we beat Sammie," I said. I dropped the gun bag beside the table by the front door and headed for the kitchen and my stash of sweet tea. I could use one after the day I'd had.

"I'mma go change out of this," Cassy said. She grabbed the gun bag off the floor and headed upstairs.

I was too tired to go up and change. I let Needles out into the yard, then sat with my head leaning against the back of the couch—I fell asleep right away. The sound of the doorbell ringing, followed by a knock, woke me up.

I hushed Needles, who was now closed up in the kitchen, then pushed off the blanket Cassy must have laid over me and dragged my feet to the front door. Sammie's bag was on the bottom step alongside the twins' shoes. I really must have been out if I didn't hear them get home.

I knew it would be Antonio on the other side of the door. It was his signature greeting. I glanced at the clock over the stove when I paused to settle Needles down. It was going on eleven thirty p.m. Wow, yeah, I missed the last two hours.

I pulled open the front door, and there he was on the other side of the storm door. He looked as exhausted as I felt. I didn't have it in my heart to be mean to him when all our defenses were down, so instead, I pushed open the storm door to where he stood looking at me.

"Are you coming in or are you going to just stand there?" I asked when he didn't move.

He stepped inside and immediately wrapped me in his arms. I didn't know what that was about, but I was too tired to push him away. Plus, I really just needed a hug right then. I wrapped my arms around his waist and laid my head on his shoulder. The storm door closed behind us and shut the night sounds outside.

After a few minutes he pulled back, and I got another look at him. At least I tried to, but in the next second he was kissing me—and it was the good kind. The butterflies took flight in my stomach, and I was the same sixteen-year-old girl again, experiencing my first kiss with him.

No sooner had I settled in to enjoy it than he pulled away. But before I could complain, he dug his hands into my hair and hauled me back in for another one. This one was the opposite of the first. Where the first was tender and sweet, this one was raw and emotional. We fought to see who would win an invisible fight we didn't know we were having.

He let go abruptly, and I put my hand against the wall to hold myself up. My head was spinning with all the emotions and movement.

"I love you, Laci. You exasperate me and irritate me, and God knows I want to wring your neck more than I do anyone else's, but damnit, Laci, I love you."

My mouth fell open in shock, and before I could think, let alone say anything, he was out the door and in his car. What just happened? Where did that come from? With no answer to those questions, I dragged myself upstairs, brushed my teeth, used the bathroom, then crawled into bed.

I disrupted Boo on her pillow next to my head, but she took it in stride. I didn't know what happened to cause Antonio to react the way he did, but secretly, I was glad he came. Now, after all this time, I knew he still loved me, but I never got the chance to tell him I still loved him, too.

Chapter Five

"Yesh?" It was six in the morning, and I was barely awake. Who would call at this time of the morning?

"Did I wake you up, Laci?" Kristen Waters came across the line with the cheery voice of someone on their third cup of coffee, or in my case, their first swig of morning sweet tea.

"Ish okay." I stumbled through my words. "I'm getting up." I didn't move.

"I'm sorry. I just wanted to let you know I set up a time for you to meet with the other officers in the spouse's club."

I pushed myself up in bed. "I'm awake. What time and where?"

"Ruby can't meet today but will get back to me when she can. The rest are all set to meet today at the coffee shop where you and I met. I hope that's okay."

"It's fine. What time?"

"Ten o'clock this morning," she said.

"Thank you for doing this for me, Mrs. Waters. I appreciate it."

"Oh, hon, you can call me Kristen if you want to."

"Oh, well, thank you…Kristen."

We hung up, and I hopped out of bed, scaring Boo in the process. I jumped in the shower and scheduled my day in my head. I could get work done here in my home office, so I didn't need to get on the road.

I stepped out of the shower, and someone knocked on my bedroom door. I wrapped myself in a towel then went and opened it and found Sammie on the other side.

"Hey." I smiled down at Ana, who was yanking on the front of my towel. I tucked myself in and picked her up. Ryan was yanking on Sammie's other hand while she tried to talk to me.

"Can I borrow your car this morning? I would have asked you last night, but you were plum worn out, and I didn't want to wake you. I know you have to get to work this morning, but I thought we could work something out."

"I'm working from home this morning, so you're free to use it. I do need it no later than nine thirty, though. Does that work?"

"Oh, yes, that's perfect. Thank you. Come on, Ana, we gotta go get ready for school."

Ana had her own feelings about that and crossed her little arms over her chest and said, "No."

"Excuse me, little miss?" Sammie said. She got Ryan loose from her other hand and took Ana from my arms. "You don't tell Momma no, Ana. You know that."

Ana didn't like that and started crying and reaching for me. It was too much for me to handle because I would start crying too in an instant where she was concerned. I closed my door, but I could still hear Ana crying from Sammie's room.

Once I changed for the day, I went downstairs and grabbed my sweet tea from the fridge, and let Needles outside. I joined him but sat while he ran, sniffing everything in the yard. Out of the corner of my eye,

Boo stuck her paw through the hanging screen, quickly followed by the rest of her. She rubbed against my leg on her way to the grass, where she rolled around before settling on a patch to snack on. I hoped she kept it down this time.

Sammie and the twins were gone when I went back inside, and Cassy was sitting at the dining room table with her laptop in front of her.

"What are you working on?" I asked.

"Tryin' to find a law school."

"Anything in particular striking your fancy?" I asked.

"Mmm. Well, seein' as how there's only two in Maryland, I don' have a lot to choose from."

"There's only two? In the whole state?"

"Mmmhmmm. University of Maryland and University of Baltimore. Both of which only got fifty-five-ish percent acceptance rate."

"Have you taken the LSAT yet?"

"Not yet. I'm still studying."

"When do you plan on taking it?" I asked. You could study forever and keep putting it off for fear of never passing it.

"Sometime soon if I wanna start in January. Tha's the goal."

"Well, let me know what I can do to help you. Oh, and Cassy…" I waited for her to look up. "You can do this. I know you can."

Her eyes filled up—surprising the hell out of me. "Thank you, Laci."

****

I settled in at my desk and got down to filtering emails on my work computer. Halfway through my latest round of emails, I remembered I wanted to check Neighbor Space next to the ball fields to see if they had any cameras.

After several passes through the system, I finally landed at the security desk where I met a cheerful voice attached to a woman named Hazel Bowry.

"Well, honey, how can I help you today?" Hazel asked once all the pleasantries were exchanged.

"I'm calling to find out if you guys, by any chance, have a video camera that oversees the ball fields to the right of your center?"

"Oh, well, I'll have to look into that, because I don't right know if we do or not. Can I get your number to call you back when I get an answer?"

I really didn't want to have to call back about this or wait to hear, but I didn't have a choice. I gave her my number and asked for one in return, and she assured me it was the number to her direct line. I could only trust her word and hope she wasn't simply trying to get me off the phone.

With that done, I decided to hold my breath while I called the Harford County Sheriff's office to speak with Deputy Robinson. Part of me wanted him there, while part of me wanted to leave him to someone else. He answered once the rerouting was done.

"Deputy Robinson, Harford County Sheriff's office. How can I help you?"

"Deputy Robinson, this is Special Agent Laci Duvall. We met Sunday at the ballpark over the dead woman with the pink flamingo?"

"It's not funny, Ms. Duvall," he said.

"I wasn't laughing, Robinson," I said.

"It's Deputy Robinson, Ms. Duvall," he said.

"Okay, then it's either Major Duvall or Special Agent Duvall, Deputy Robinson."

I could practically hear him grinding his teeth over the line. I knew his type. I worked with them and recently got attacked by one. They felt women should still be barefoot at home—God forbid we're actually good at a job and, horror of horrors, dare be better than them.

"Fine. *Major* Duvall. What did you call me for?"

Was there something in the water here? What was with the emphasis? "Did you learn anything else about the dead woman or the crime scene?" I asked.

"The only thing I learned was the military takes care of their own."

"I'm sorry? I don't know what that means."

"Yes, you do," he said. "I was warned to stay far away from this investigation."

"Who warned you?" I asked.

"Some girl with a boy's name," he said.

"Wesley?" I asked. "Wesley Hanscom?"

"Yeah, that sounds about right."

"Deputy, I promise you, Captain Hanscom has no authority to tell you to stay out of this investigation. We at the OSI need your help and insight to the local area and people. I'm sorry if you were told to stay away. That is not the case here."

"Well, who are you to tell me that she's not in charge? She told me otherwise."

"Deputy, I know you are aware of the order of rankings, are you not?"

"Yes."

"Then you also know that a Major ranks above a Captain, which means I outrank her. If you need further confirmation, I will give you my boss's number, and you can speak with him if you wish. His name is Colonel Waters, and he will be more than happy to set the record straight. Do you want his number?"

"Yes, Major, I think that would be wise," he said.

I gave him Colonel Waters's phone number while silently cursing Hanscom. How dare she undermine my authority like this. I hung up with him and shot a text to Colonel Waters alerting him to the incoming phone call.

With that taken care of, I turned my sights to the interview I would be having in a couple of hours. I wanted to jot some questions down so I would be ready.

Taking a lesson from Desio, I grabbed a small notebook out of my drawer and put each person's name at the top of different pages. They would all get the same questions. How long did you know the deceased? What were your interactions with her like? How well do you know Ruby Moffat? And more along the same line.

With that ready to go, I waited for Sammie to get home, but with time ticking closer and closer to nine o'clock, my concern grew and grew. At 9:05 I couldn't take it anymore and called her.

"Laci, I know I'm late, but it's not my fault. I'm sorry about your car, but Daddy's on his way to get me. I swanny he's going to have a yard full of cars by the time this week is up."

I tried to interrupt her, really I did. But she was on a roll, and I couldn't get a word in. Finally, when she stopped to breathe, I got my chance.

"Sammie, where are you? What's happened? What do you mean sorry about my car?"

"Didn't you get my text messages? Now why in tarnation didn't that go through? I wonder. I was driving down Bird River Road because there was an accident on Pulaski I was trying to avoid when all of a sudden, out of nowhere, someone shot out of Holly Hill like their tail was on fire and ran right into the passenger front tire and quarter panel. Now, don't that beat all?"

"Sammie, I have to go. Do you have a way to get home?" I asked.

"Oh, yes, Daddy's just down the road and will be here directly."

We said our goodbyes and I dialed up Rev.

"Yellow," someone answered.

"Rev?" I asked.

"Yep, that's me. You need a ride, hon?"

"Yes, please," I said. "Do you need the address?"

"Nah, I gotcha from last night. See ya in a few."

True to his word, Rev was at my house in under ten minutes. Which left me twelve minutes to get to the coffee shop.

"How soon can we get to Golden Ring Mall?" I pulled the door shut behind me. Technically it wasn't "Golden Ring Mall" anymore—hadn't been for years. But to me, that's what it would always be.

"How soon do you need to be there?"

"Ten minutes?"

"Done."

We took off like a shot, complete with backfire and everything. If it were possible I think there was more cussing and honking than last time. He was definitely colorful, but we made it in ten minutes flat. We pulled up to the shop, and Rev slammed on the brakes. I steadied myself on the dash and laughed. That was quite the experience.

"You need me to hang around and wait for you to get done?" he asked.

"Sure, that would be great. Am I keeping you from other rides?"

"Nah, it's my day off," he said.

"Wait, what?"

"It's okay. I like you. So, I don't mind."

I shook my head and climbed from the car, where I braced myself on the passenger door while my legs firmed up under me. Rev rolled out and went into the bagel store next door.

I stepped inside and looked for a group of two women and one man. I don't know why I thought that would be easy, but the shop was full of that scenario. I never thought to ask Kristen what to look for. *Shit.*

I strolled through the shop, and in the back corner, at the table where I sat with Anne Carson, was a group of three people with their heads together. One wore an Aberdeen Iron Birds shirt, so I took a chance and approached their table.

When I got closer, I recognized the one in the shirt as Candice Landis from the day at the park. The man must be Miles and Haylee was the other woman.

"Candice?" I asked the group.

"Yes?" She stood and extended her hand. I met it over the table for a reasonably firm shake. The others at the table got up as well, and I shook their hands in order from Haylee to Miles.

"Thank you for agreeing to meet me," I said.

"Of course," Candice said. "We want to do whatever we can to find out who did this."

The others nodded in agreement.

"Well, first, can you tell me how long did you know Jill Westfall?" I asked.

"I'll start," Candice said after a moment's hesitation from the group. "We were stationed with Jill and her husband about eight years ago, and then we were assigned here last summer. Jill was excited we were coming because she said she finally knew someone else."

"Is that what she said?" Miles asked. "I've known Jill since high school and was here before she arrived. When she first saw me here, it was like we were long lost best friends—when we were anything but that."

I turned to Haylee to see what she had to say. She opened her mouth once, then closed it without saying anything. I guess she found what she wanted to say because she then spoke in a low voice.

"I knew her the least of everyone then because I just met her when we moved here a few months ago."

"I thought you told me you guys were stationed together at your last post?" Miles asked. When Haylee didn't elaborate, he shrugged, and I moved on.

"Did you all get along with each other?" I asked.

"It was hard to get along with Jill," Miles said. "You never knew what her ulterior motive was, and trust me, she always had one."

"See, I disagree—" Candice said.

"Shocker," Miles interrupted.

Candice stopped and froze him in place with a glare. Or rather, she would have if Miles cared enough. I suddenly saw who was Team Jill and who was Team Ruby. Haylee's preference was still a mystery.

"What was she like on a day-to-day basis?" I

asked. I was trying to keep us moving and not at each other's throats.

"She was sweet," Candice said. I saw Miles roll his eyes. "She *was*, Miles."

"Yeah, to you," he said. "But being the only man on the board, I had a different experience than you did. She was a real b-word to anyone who dared contradict her. I made that mistake once, and she blacklisted me from every committee. Why do you think it was so delicious when I was voted onto the board this year? There wasn't a damn thing she could do about it either, and you can bet your boots I enjoyed letting her know it."

"What about you, Haylee?" I asked.

"My interactions with her were minimal," she said. She seemed very quiet and fearful of saying something wrong. "I only saw her at board meetings and our get-togethers. Our paths didn't cross that much."

"Were you privy to any of the things she said about Ruby Moffat?" I asked. I figured with Miles's dislike of Jill I should be able to get something out of him. I didn't have to wait long.

"Oh, her hatred of Ruby was legendary." Miles practically rubbed his hands together with glee.

"Why did she hate her so much?" I asked.

"It all started last year when promotions came out. Jill was *sure* that Noah would be promoted below the zone. I mean she had a banner made up with his new rank and everything. So, when he came home, and he didn't get it. She. Was. Pissed.

"She found out Ruby's husband, Damian, was promoted below the zone when Ruby came to the group asking about having their yard flocked. Having your yard flocked means the spouse's club will take a bunch of pink plastic flamingos and put them all over your yard as a way of celebrating with you. Anyway, Jill had a meltdown and said no, the club wouldn't do it.

"Instead of begging Jill to concede, Ruby went to Amelia Carter, the wife of the Garrison Commander, and told her what happened. Let's just say Ruby got her flamingos and Jill got a talking to."

"Is that your all's take on it?" I asked. I wanted to see what the other two thought.

"More or less," Candice said.

Haylee nodded her head.

"So, because of that, Jill started spreading lies about Ruby," Miles said. "She hated her with a passion usually reserved for cheer moms."

"That's it? That's what all this is based on?" I asked. "I don't get it. That's so little."

"You obviously don't deal much with military spouses," Miles said, and Candice nodded her head. At least they agreed for once. "It's no joke when you hear spouses wear their husband's rank. They wield it like a sword and take down people they feel are beneath them. When Ruby's husband got promoted, it upset the balance of their whole dynamic, and Jill knew it. Ruby didn't care, but Jill did, and Ruby's lack of concern made Jill even more angry."

"It's true," Candice said. "Not only that, but Jill joined because she wanted to usurp anyone whose spouse was ranked higher than hers. She felt it gave her an edge. When Damian was promoted, she went a little nuts for a while. I really thought she was pulling through it until the last incident before she was killed."

"Uh-oh," I said. "What was the last incident?"

Miles, Haylee, and Candice looked at each other before Miles nodded his head. I guess that meant Candice could continue.

"Jill rented a billboard on Pulaski and basically advertised that Ruby slept with their husband's boss. She doctored up an image to make it look like Ruby and Henry were caught kissing. The image was shot from a distance to make it look credible."

"Oh shit," I said. "What did Ruby do?"

"She denied it, of course, but the damage was done," Miles said.

"How long ago was this?" I asked.

"A couple weeks," Haylee said.

"Did no one go to the base commander about her?" I asked. "How was she allowed free rein to bully whoever she wanted?"

"Up until the billboard, it was all hearsay," Miles said.

"Amelia Carter was in the process of stripping her of her position," Candice said.

"Really?" Miles seemed surprised by the news, but Candice and Haylee nodded in confirmation.

"Is the billboard still up?" I asked.

"Yes, I saw it on my way down here," Haylee said.

It looked like Rev and I were in for a field trip.

Chapter Six

Rev zipped up Pulaski, and I swear we approached Mach One at some point. He really had no concept of speed.

"So, what do you do?" he asked.

"I work for the Air Force Office of Special Investigations," I said. "Kinda like the FBI, but for the Air Force."

He whistled. "You on a case right now?"

I nodded and recalled my last question to the group.

"Where was Ruby during the softball game?" I asked.

The three looked at each other, but ultimately they agreed they saw her before the game began, but no one saw her after the beginning of the first inning. This did not bode well for Ruby's alibi.

My attention was brought back to the present by an upcoming billboard. You could see it a half-mile away. The red A was supposed to stand for the *Scarlet Letter,* I imagined. Overlapping the ten-foot A was a nine-foot image of a couple in an intimate embrace. I didn't know what Ruby or Colonel Chandler looked like, so I couldn't tell if this was them or not. Their faces were evident but a little fuzzy in the picture. If you knew who they were, you would know it was them in the picture, but if they were strangers to you, you would have a hard time identifying them here.

Rev whistled again when we got out to look at it. The cars flowed by us on Pulaski, and occasionally, the wind and noise would kick up from a tractor trailer.

"Now, who would do something like this? Ain't that red A from a book?" he asked.

"Yep," I said. "*The Scarlet Letter*."

While we stood there, a work van pulled up between us and the sign and started unloading. It looked like we got there at the right time. I took out my phone and snapped a few pictures. I walked around the van until I was as close as I could get and snapped a few more, including some close-ups of their faces.

"All right, Rev, I'm ready to go."

When we got home, I invited him in for lunch. I figured I owed him since it was his day off. He looked around while I grabbed sandwich stuff. Cassy joined us in the kitchen, so I added another one to the pile.

"What'd you learn this morning?" Cassy asked.

I filled her in on everything while Rev listened and asked questions. I didn't stop him because I hoped he might ask something that would help.

"So, no one knows where this Ruby person was when the other one was killed? She's also supposed to be the one on the sign we just seen?" Rev asked.

"Yes," I said.

"What do the locals think?" Cassy asked.

"Oh, that's another thing. I spoke with Deputy Robinson this morning and guess who warned him off?"

"Desio?" Cassy asked.

"Nope. Captain Wesley Hanscom. So, not only did I have to soothe his ruffled feathers, but I also had to let

Colonel Waters know that she was overstepping her boundaries. Oh, and she was with Desio when I spoke with him yesterday."

"Do what now?"

"Yeah, she told Waters she was going to interview someone about a case she was working on without actually telling him who it was."

"Uh-oh," Rev said.

"Yeah, you have no idea how angry I am at this woman. Oh, that reminds me. I haven't heard back yet from Hazel at the Neighbor Space to see if she has video of the ball fields."

"Why we gotta wait? We can just go over and look ourselves for cameras pointing in that direction." Cassy said.

"You up for it, Rev?" I asked.

"Sure, why not. It's not like I got anything better to do today. Lunch and an outing. What could be better?"

"That's the spirit," Cassy said.

We cleaned up and headed to Rev's car. I tried to snag the back, but Cassy beat me to it. Again. It didn't really bother me too much—at least I could see the end coming before it got there.

The drive up Route 40 to Edgewood was relatively uneventful if you didn't count the number of seatbelt locks and "urks" from Cassy in the back.

At Neighbor Space we unloaded, and I was ushered to the front of the line to ask for Hazel Bowry. We were told she was at lunch and would be back in about half an hour. We then went outside to see what we could find—if anything.

The east side of the building faced the ball fields and the brick building that housed the bathrooms. The yellow tape was off the bathroom, so we decided to take a look. Rev waited outside while Cassy and I snooped around the murder scene.

The stall door was removed from the toilet where Jill was found. The room didn't smell like it had been deep cleaned, so maybe we would find something.

"I'll take the trash and sink area if you wanna take the john," Cassy said.

"No, I don't want the stall. You know it makes me sick to my stomach. Why don't you do it?"

"Consider it immersion therapy," Cassy said.

"How the hell you know what immersion therapy is?" I asked.

"What? I can' have layers?"

I crossed my arms on my chest and stared her down.

"I learned it after a 'critical incident' with the BPD last year."

"What was the incident?" I asked.

"Quit stalling and get to work," she said.

I eyed her a little bit longer, but she turned her back to me and began her search. I went about my own task and willed myself not to remember what I saw the last time. It took a few minutes, but I found something.

"Cass, does this look like a bullet hole to you?"

About three feet over the lid of the toilet was a hole in the wall. It was empty, but the circumference and blow out around the hole looked like it was recent.

"Yeah, looks like a 9 mm," she said.

"That's what I was thinking, too," I said.

"There ain' no way to tell if it was from this weekend or not, though."

"I wonder if Robinson would tell us if we asked."

"Does it matter if it was from her or not?" Cassy asked.

"It could point to intent. Dale said whoever did it was determined to kill her; this would reinforce that theory."

We exited the bathroom and looked for Rev, but he was nowhere to be found. On the way back to Neighbor Space, we saw him along the side of the building and the woods surrounding it. We met him halfway down the sidewalk.

"See any cameras?" I asked.

"There's a couple of them." He turned, and we followed him back the way he came. "Up there's one." He pointed to the eaves, and you could plainly see a black box with a lens sticking out of it.

"Is that the only one?"

"Only one I seen so far, but I didn't make it all the way to the end of the building. I'm not sure the angle on this one will do you any good when it comes down to it, though. It *might* catch a corner of the building, but I doubt it. These are for security around the building, not so much for distance. If you get something, it might be fuzzy as hell."

We retraced our steps from the end of the line of buildings and back inside to see if Hazel had returned. The front desk worker pointed us toward her office, and we received an order to come in when we knocked on her door. The tiny little woman that greeted us was a surprise—I swear I could have fit her in my pocket.

"Well, hello there. How can I help you today?" she asked.

"Hi, Ms. Bowry, I spoke to you this morning on the phone. About the cameras?"

Her face cleared, and she jumped out of her chair with a hand extended. "That's right. You're the one looking for the camera footage? Oh, my, you are a big one." She stopped next to Rev and looked straight up. It was comical. There must have been at least three feet separating their heights.

"Yes, ma'am. That's what my momma always said to me, too." Rev grinned at her.

"Now, I done told Security I would be by to get a copy of the footage from Sunday. You all just wait here, and I'll be right back."

"Do you get that a lot?" I asked Rev.

"Only from small people," he said.

"How tall are you anyways?" Cassy asked. "I mean, I'm six foot even, and you got me by a head at least."

"Last I was checked, I was six-foot-eight," he said.

"Yeah, you are a big one." Hazel was back. "Security said they got what they could off of it, but at the distance and angle of the camera there wasn't a whole lot."

She handed me a thumb drive, and I thanked her for her time. It looked like Rev was right about the camera, which was a bummer.

We walked outside with the intent to go back home, but something told me we should see if we could get an appointment with the post commander, General Fields at Aberdeen. I called Colonel Waters to see if he could get me in, and while we waited to hear from him, we dropped in at the donut place on Route 40 in Edgewood. We'd been there no more than fifteen minutes when Colonel Waters texted me that I had an appointment with her in thirty minutes. We currently sat twenty-five minutes away, and that didn't account for traffic.

"All right, Rev, do your thing, but just don't get caught."

We made it in twenty minutes, which included getting everyone signed in. Once on post, we made our way to Building 305, which served as headquarters. It's been years since I was there, and the memories came flooding back. The burger chain was still in place next to the Post Exchange (PX) which was across the street from the commissary they built in the '90s.

The section that used to handle the mustard gas was down Aberdeen Boulevard by the old personnel offices. You could follow the water on your left to Woodpecker Point, which held a great view of the northern Chesapeake Bay. We didn't have time for a grand tour, so I just pointed stuff out to Rev and Cassy en route to meet General Fields.

"Good morning, Captain," I greeted the Executive Assistant in the outer office. "I have an appointment with General Fields. I'm Special Agent Major Laci Duvall—these are my associates, but they'll be waiting out here."

I turned and gave Cassy and Rev a Cheshire smile. I know I changed the plan on them last minute, but I didn't want my first meeting with the general to be unorthodox. Let her learn on her own that I didn't always play by the rules.

"Good morning, Major. Yes, she's expecting you." The captain held the door open for me to enter General Fields's office.

I was pleasantly surprised by the warm greeting I received from General Fields. She approached, and I shook her hand. She was a petite woman with sandy-colored hair, which was graying at the temples.

"Major, what can I do for you today?"

"Thank you for giving me an audience this morning, General. I shouldn't be long. I'm investigating the murder that took place at the softball game over the weekend. Can you tell me anything about the Moffats and the Westfalls?"

"Lieutenant Colonel Moffat and Major Westfall are deployed together, and Major Westfall is en route to Aberdeen and should be here anytime. We're trying to get Colonel Moffat back as well. They neither one have children and are neighbors in base housing, and until recently, they served under Colonel Chandler, who retired last month. Their new commander isn't here yet."

"Did you know Mrs. Moffat is under suspicion of killing Mrs. Westfall?"

"I've heard the rumors, yes, but they are baseless at this point, aren't they?" she asked.

"Yes, ma'am, as far as I know they are. Do you know anything about the billboard on Pulaski?"

"I never saw the billboard myself, but it was brought to my attention, yes. It's supposed to be removed ASAP."

"When I left the area this morning, it was being replaced. Do you know who paid to have it put up?"

"Major, it's only a rumor. I don't have anything else to say about who would do such a thing."

"What do you know that isn't a rumor, General?" It was time to cut to the chase and get a straight answer. Evasive maneuvers were fine and good in the theater, but when someone was dead, there were things I needed to know yesterday.

"These two families have a history. Lieutenant Colonel Moffat and Mrs. Westfall grew up together and dated all through high school. They're local and went to Edgewood High School. Mrs. Westfall ended things with Colonel Moffat when he shipped out for basic training. Colonel Moffat met his wife at his first assignment at Fort Bragg. They dated for a few years before they married around ten years ago. She is currently expecting their first child."

"Oh, I didn't know that," I said.

"Yes, well it's not being bandied about because she experienced a miscarriage a few years ago."

"Yes, ma'am. I understand," I said. In other words, I was not to repeat it at any cost.

"Major and Mrs. Westfall met when he was stationed here at Aberdeen the first time around eight years ago. I believe Mrs. Moffat introduced them."

"Were they friends?" I asked.

"It appeared that way from the outside," General Fields said. "If you asked anyone who knew them, they would probably say yes, but with the goings on in the spouse's club, I may need to change my opinion."

"Yes, General. Would you be able to set up an appointment with Major Westfall when he arrives? Also, Lieutenant Colonel Moffat when he's home?"

She pressed the button on her phone for her exec and instructed him to make an appointment for me with the two men when they could. With nothing left to do but wait, I said goodbye to General Fields and left.

"I'll be in touch." General Fields walked us to the door to the hallway, and we said our goodbyes.

She'd given me a lot to think about, and I needed

to get home and take notes on this meeting while preparing for the one to come.

Chapter Seven

With no cars to take me anywhere the next morning, I settled into my home office to get some work done. Sammie's dad came and picked her and the twins up to take to daycare. Cassy was in her room scheduling her LSATs while also looking for a class on the preparation that would need to go into taking it. I didn't have any doubts that she would ace them.

My phone pinged in the silence and notified me that General Fields's office had succeeded in setting up an appointment with me and the two men tomorrow morning. It looked like they'd both arrived home.

I created a new document to sort out my thoughts, but it turned out I didn't have any thoughts. I was winging it. I remembered the thumb drive and grabbed it from my bag on the table by the front door.

Clicking through all the files, I finally landed on the video I needed. Two downloaded software apps so I could watch it later—I finally got the file open. *Damnit,* I couldn't see the bathrooms from this angle—just like everyone told me. I pressed on in the hopes that something would stand out. The time stamp in the corner revealed it was too early for our softball game, so I returned to the main file. I cycled through a few more videos before I landed on the time I needed.

I realized whoever did this could have arrived at any point the morning of the murder. Dale gave us a wide point of reference for time of death, and the spouse's club members weren't able to contribute to when they saw Jill last.

Cars came and went through the parking lot. Some people filtered onto the ball fields, and some made their way into Neighbor Space. I didn't know what Ruby Moffat looked like, so I was shooting in the dark where she was concerned.

I closed down the video and opened another. The camera captured the left field player in the softball game and part of the third basemen. Every now and then, I could see Captain Hanscom performing some feat on the ballfield.

Antonio pulled in with his car and parked facing the ball field. He got out, and Hanscom, who was in the process of running behind third base, stopped in her tracks and the ball dropped in front of her. So, I wasn't imagining things there.

The remaining videos were more of the same—cars in and people out. I wished I knew what Ruby looked like. I needed more information, so I picked up my phone and dialed Deputy Robinson's office.

"Robinson," he said once I finally reached him. It was almost as bad as trying to get customer service at my cell phone carrier.

"Good morning, Deputy. This is Major Duvall. I was wondering if you had any witness statements from the ball game this weekend?"

"We have a few, Major. Did that Captain not give them to you?"

I saw red. Immediately. "No sir, she did not. Maybe it's better if we did this in person from now on. Could you email me what you sent to her?" I rattled off my address, and he agreed to email me and only me from then on out. We also agreed to a meeting that afternoon. While I waited for them to show up in my inbox I tried to breathe and bring down my temper. This was the last straw.

"What?" Colonel Waters really didn't know how he sounded on the other end. At this point in his career, I doubt he even cared.

"Colonel Waters, I will not have Captain Hanscom interfering anymore in my investigation. She is going behind my back and speaking to people involved in the case. It's creating friction between myself, the people I'm supposed to be interviewing, and those I'm working with to solve the case."

I went into specifics, and with each item ticked off, Colonel Waters's exclamations got more and more colorful. Finally, when he was ready to erupt, I finished my laundry list of complaints against her. I was not one to whine about my job, but enough was enough already.

"I will get this taken care of, Major." There was a long pause. "Nope. I'm not going to ask for a progress report. Mrs. Waters is hounding me for answers, and I want to be able to say, I don't know. Let me know if Hanscom gives you any more trouble after today."

We signed off, and I opened the email from Robinson. The message was vague and didn't touch on the kind of information I needed from him. I was glad I set up some face-to-face time. Next, I texted Rev, who agreed to pick me up around one for my 1:30 p.m. meeting with Robinson.

****

"Where you goin'?" Cassy asked. My bag was slung over my shoulder while I stood in the kitchen, finishing off an odd bottle of sweet tea from the fridge. Rev would be there any minute.

"I have a meeting with Deputy Robinson. Do you want to come along for the ride?"

"Damn skippy."

She raced back up the steps, and someone knocked on the front door. I opened it and found Rev filling the doorway with a smile on his face.

"You ready, hon?"

"Just waiting on Cas—"

"I'm here." Cassy jogged down the hallway and joined us when we went outside, and I locked the door.

Once in the car, I gave him directions to the sheriff's office. "I would suggest driving a touch slower the closer we get, Rev. I wouldn't want to give them a target if I were you."

He did as I suggested, and it was surreal. Almost like I was driving with a stranger. We got there with no screeching when we stopped. It was eerie—when the hell had I grown used to his driving?

"That was weird." Cassy spoke my thoughts when we got out.

"I know, right," I said.

Once through the automatic doors, I approached the desk of the perky receptionist—who beamed at all of us.

"I'm here to see Deputy Robinson. He's expecting me," I said.

"Slay—let me check."

"*Sleigh?*" I turned to Cassy. "Like Santa's sleigh?"

Cassy laughed, and the receptionist gave us the side-eye.

"Damn, Laci, dontchu know slang? It's s-l-a-y.

Like, you slay me. Or you slay that outfit. Meaning you totally killed."

Five minutes and a lesson in slang terminology later, Robinson arrived. With a glance at Rev, he touched the gun at his hip and juggled the laptop in the other. That was weird. I looked Rev over, but he didn't seem threatening to me. Khaki shorts, black T-shirt with a kitten riding a unicorn, socks, and black boots. Looked normal to me.

"Deputy Robinson, this is Rev. Rev, this is Deputy Robinson," I said. "Is there some place we can talk? Do you mind if we all sit in on this meeting?" See— unconventional.

He nodded, turned, and proceeded down the hall. We followed him, and one glance into a room revealed a layout similar to a classroom. Halfway down, he pushed open a door on the left and led us to a conference table with assorted chairs around it.

We each took a spot, and no sooner were we all seated than across the table, Cassy's feet flew up in the air, and she almost overturned in her chair. She would have, too, if Rev hadn't been next to her and righted her before she fell over. Once back in place, she casually clasped her hands on the table in front of her.

"How can I help you?" Robinson asked.

"What can you tell me about the investigation? I read through your email, and there was a lot missing. Is there anything else you want to add now that I'm here? Have any witnesses come forward?"

He placed the laptop on the conference table and typed a bit. I grabbed my notebook from my bag, Desio's influence, and pulled the pen from the spiral.

"The witnesses I spoke with were Mrs. Haylee

Bishop, Mrs. Candice Landis, and a few players from the softball match. The players all said they weren't paying attention to the bathrooms, so they didn't see anything off.

"I reviewed the footage from the camera on the roof of the building, but it only captures part of left field. There are trees blocking the bathrooms and no cameras are directed toward it."

"The footage I saw was the same," I said. "What have you discovered about the victim?"

"The Army has been pretty hush-hush on her and her husband. Do you have anything you can share?" he asked.

I went through my notes and filtered out what was hearsay and stuck with the facts. On my second run-through, I warned him it was gossip but listed what I'd learned from the officers of the spouse's club. He asked questions, and I did my best to answer where I could, but I only knew what I was told.

"Do you see similarities to any cases you might have here in the county?" Cassy asked.

"Mmmm, not really," Robinson said. "This one is unique in the scope of the way she was killed and where. How did no one hear the shot? Did anyone see someone with a pink flamingo?"

"So, no one seen any of that?" Cassy asked.

"Not that they reported to me," Robinson said. "We all know whoever did this could be lying. Someone there killed this woman, and from what you've told me about the spouse's club, there were many who had reason to."

"True, I think we need to focus on the spouse's club members," I said. "It sounds to me like Jill made more enemies than she did friends. Dale told me about the bullet in her. Did you guys find any more evidence in the bathroom?"

"There was another bullet hole in the wall behind her, but with no bullet it could be from something else. Edgewood is working on cleaning up their image, but this particular area has run the gamut from peaceful to violent. Will you be needing our assistance further?"

"Oh, yes. I know we didn't get off on the right foot, but it's never the intention of OSI to take over an investigation. We work with you guys, especially when a case rides the line like this one does. It's going to take all of us to find who did this."

He walked us to the front entrance, where we said goodbye. I held my hand out for him to shake, and he met mine. It was a new start.

"From here on out, you deal only with me, Robinson," I said. "You can contact me anytime, and I hope I can do the same."

He nodded, then turned and went back inside. I stared after him—hoping and praying this would be an easy alliance.

With Cassy and Rev waiting in the car, I hopped in the front seat while wondering what my next step should be.

"Where to, hon?" Rev asked.

"What do you think, Cassy? I'm fresh out of ideas."

"You got the home address on that Jill woman? I say we go see the neighborhood and talk to the other neighbors. Maybe they know somethin'."

"Great idea. I'll text Colonel Waters and see if he knows it. Regardless, we can still cruise the neighborhoods while we wait for him."

Cassy and Rev's visitor passes were still good, so we made it on post without incident. Colonel Waters's text with Ruby's address came through once we got on post. The row of tanks that used to greet you just beyond the front gate had been moved to Virginia. It costs a pretty penny to move tanks for no reason.

At the stoplight by the commissary, we hooked a right onto Aberdeen Boulevard and stayed there until it turned into Civil Road, then took a left to Plum Point. There were a bunch of one-ways, and Rev stopped more than once to make sure he didn't go down the wrong way. That's all we needed was to explain ourselves to the MPs before we were ready.

These were the historic homes, and everyone wanted to live in them. The loop led to the Chesapeake Bay, and the houses were only on one side of the road. This meant there were no neighbors in front of you or behind you, just next to you. We exited the loop to catch Ground Road, where houses lined both sides of the street. In the old days your rank and name were displayed on the front door for all to see. With the mingling of retirees, civilians, and contractors, you didn't see them as much.

I had Rev park on the shoulder when we reached the middle of the road. Ruby's house was directly beside us, which meant Jill's was to the left. There was about thirty yards between the stone cottage-style houses, which were carbon copies of each other. Ruby's windows held flower boxes, and a wreath hung on her front door. A dog lead was attached to the tree in the front yard of Jill's house, but it was empty.

Purely by coincidence an older woman two houses

up from Jill's, opposite of Ruby's, exited her front door with a dog on a leash. I seized the opportunity and got out of the car and approached her.

"Good afternoon," I said. "My name is Special Agent Major Laci Duvall. I'm with Air Force OSI. Can I ask you a couple questions?"

She looked like she instantly regretted stepping outside her front door. Her shoulders sagged, and she cast her eyes to the grass beneath us.

"It's all very sad," she said. "I've known Jill for a couple years now. We weren't friends, she was rather hard to get to know, but we waved when we saw each other on the street. You know?"

"I do know, yes," I said. "I'm sorry to have to ask questions when this is all so new, but the sooner we get information the sooner we can find who did this. Can you tell me anything about her daily routine or habits?"

"She would run every morning with their dog, Sweets. I don't know who has him now what with all that's happened and her husband not getting back until tonight. She had family in the area, but from what she said, they don't sound like they were on good terms, if you know what I mean.

"She had the spouse's club, which she was in charge of. It was her whole world. She and Noah didn't have any children. She let slip once that she'd had a pregnancy terminated when he was out of town for training. I don't know if she ever told him; I never asked."

I was writing as fast as I could, but there was a lot to unpack from this woman.

"Could you tell me your name?" I asked.

"Oh, why, I'm Betsey Zimmer. My husband is a

retired Sergeant Major. We were lucky enough to get this place. It's my dream home, and I don't have to worry about upkeep outside and inside. It's heaven."

"Did Jill have any negative interactions with anyone recently that you know of?" I asked.

"No, not that I know of."

"Did she have any close friends? Someone who came over just to hang out with Jill or even with her and Noah?"

"Mmmm, the spouse's club people would come over for their meetings once a month. She was supposed to have General Fields and her husband over, but it was canceled at the last minute. This was around Christmas, mind you, so not recently. Other than that, I didn't really see her mingle with anyone. She didn't come to any of the neighborhood gatherings we had. Kept to herself despite Noah coming out and visiting."

"Did Jill feel unsafe here in this neighborhood?" I asked.

"Well, I can't say I know the answer to that. Should she have felt unsafe? In light of her being killed, should I feel unsafe? Oh dear, I hadn't thought of that." She began wringing her hands and winding the dog's leash around her fingers. Her fingertips turned red with her efforts.

"I'm sure there's nothing to be worried about for you here, Mrs. Zimmer. I just have one last question. How well did Jill and Noah get along?"

"Why, I guess as fine as anyone can when you're in the military. They had their arguments, but it wasn't anything any different from the rest of us, you know?"

"How do you know they argued?"

"Well, let's just say they weren't shy about airing

their dirty laundry in the backyard."

"Thank you for your time, Mrs. Zimmer. I appreciate you talking with me. Here's my card if you think of anything else."

"Oh, glad I could help. I hope you catch whoever did this. Such a horrible thing to happen to such a nice family."

When I got to the car, Cassy got out, took me by the elbow, and led me across the street to the house on the other side of Ruby's. I assumed there was a reason, so I went along with her. When we reached the sidewalk heading to the house, we stopped.

"Pretend we havin' a conversation out here."

"Okay, does this mean you can't tell me what it is we're waiting for right now?" I asked.

"Not yet." Her eyes were covered with sunglasses, which she pulled up just then so she could glance at the house behind us. She looked back at me and shook her head.

"Do you suspect someone in the house?"

"They watchin' while you were talking with the old woman. Was she any help?"

"She let some interesting information slip, and I don't think she knew the significance of it. Things like Jill secretly terminating a pregnancy and her husband and her having arguments and fights in the backyard. It's always interesting to me how people change their tune when speaking about the person after they're dead versus when they were alive. In the span of one conversation, she went from knowing nothing to verbal diarrhea in a matter of minutes."

"I know whatchu mean," Cassy said. "I'm done waitin' for this woman. Come on."

I trailed after her as she marched up the front steps and knocked on the door of the cottage. We waited about a minute before Cassy knocked again. When no one came this time, she stepped off the porch and around the side of the house. She was tall enough to see over the hedges into the backyard and waved me over.

" 'Scuse me," Cassy called over the hedges into the backyard. A few seconds later, the back door slammed shut.

"You go round front and see if they tryin' to leave," Cassy said.

Sure enough, when I got to the front, someone was quietly closing the door. In her hand was the leash to a Rottweiler. The large dog took one look at me and shot off the top step. Now, I'm not one to run from dogs, but I admit I tried to. This was over a hundred pounds of muscle with me in his crosshairs—I never stood a chance. Before I got very far, he pushed me off my feet and was licking me all over the face.

I must have screamed because Cassy burst from the side of the house like the demons of hell were on her heels. She was ready to tackle the woman on the other end of the dog's leash. Bits of bushes and twigs flew in the air and settled on the grass in her wake. Rev was out of his car and approaching us while speaking gently to the dog.

"Sweets, no," the woman said.

"Are you okay?" Rev asked from behind me. I nodded my head, but my focus was on the woman with Jill's dog. It was Haylee Bishop—the secretary for the spouse's club.

"This is Jill's dog, isn't it?" I asked.

"Yes, but I didn't steal him." A look of horror

crossed her face. "My husband, Dan, messaged Jill's husband and asked if it would help if we took Sweets for a while. Until all of this was taken care of."

I sat cross-legged on the ground with the Rottweiler's ass firmly planted in my lap. This guy wasn't moving anytime soon. I reached up and rubbed his ears between my fingers. They felt like Needles's ears—nice and velvety.

"Do you want to tell me again how well you knew Jill?" I asked.

She bit her lip and looked at Sweets. "I wasn't lying when I said I didn't know her very well. I saw you talking to Mrs. Zimmer—she lives on gossip. I don't know what she told you, but you can't believe everything you hear from her."

"I'm not going to share with you what she did or didn't say," I said. "I take and consider everything I'm told."

"Well, then you might want to consider that Mrs. Zimmer called the MPs on Jill no less than twenty times last month alone. And she was gone half the month."

"What the hell you gotta call the po-po for that many times?" Cassy asked.

"You name it, and she called. If there was anyone worse with people than Jill, it's Mrs. Zimmer."

"Was Jill bad with people?" I asked.

"You do remember the billboard incident, right?" Haylee placed one hand on her hip and tilted her head to the side in question. "But I think if this were a death due to bad neighbors, it would have been Mrs. Zimmer who was killed and not Jill."

Chapter Eight

"Is this Special Agent Major Laci Duvall?" A
voice cracked across my sleepy brain when I was
halfway to Aberdeen the next morning. Yes, I talked
Rev into letting me take his car without him. It didn't
take much. Just some box seats to an O's game next
month. Baltimore had their sights on the pennant, and
in the home stretch of August, every game counted.

"Yes, this is she," I said.

"Major, this is General Fields. I have some bad
news. The new CO for Major Westfall and Lieutenant
Colonel Moffat isn't here yet. He's requested the
interview be postponed until he's here and read up on
the situation."

"General, I know I don't have to remind you that
time is of the essence. The sooner we can get an
interview with the men, the better."

"I realize that, Major, but as a courtesy to the
incoming CO, I'm going to postpone the interview. I'll
be in touch."

She hung up before I could say anything else.
There was no point in going to base now, so I turned
onto Edgewood Road and headed up the hill to the high
school.

No one except Antonio knew I started high school
at Edgewood. They tore down my school a few years
ago and put in a new one. There was nothing left but

memories of the place. I slowed and pulled into the parking lot out front. It was empty since there was still a month before school started.

I didn't like to think about that time of my life. What was past was past. My sister Mellissa left before the ink on her diploma was dry. She couldn't wait to leave the tortured halls of the school.

With a sigh, I hooked a right onto Willoughby Beach Road. My intent was to go sit at Flying Point Park for a little while. Maybe the bay air would clear my head and ease the ache in my chest.

With a left on Flying Point Road, I stayed until I reached Kennard, which took me into the park, where I got out and sat at a picnic table. There were a few sailboats out on the water trying to coax a breeze from the heavy humid air. I wished I'd stopped at the convenience store by my house and picked up the largest sweet tea they had, but I didn't think about it until now.

I pulled out my phone and dialed.

"Desio," he said.

"Hi, Antonio," I said.

"What's wrong?" he asked.

I forced a laugh. "What makes you think anything is wrong?"

"Laci, you never call me unless something's wrong."

"Well, maybe I'm trying something new. You know. Like how you are with cursing now."

"Laci—"

I sensed his tone and dropped it. "I'm out at Flying Point Park," I said.

Silence.

"What's going on?" he asked.

I caught him up on the case and the dead ends and the interview cancelation. I included the issue I was having with Wesley and her continuous quest to take over my case.

"Laci, it sounds like she just wants to be included in the investigation. The times I've talked with her, she—"

"Why did you talk with her?" This was news to me. Silence. "Desio. When did you talk to her and why?"

"She called me the other day to ask me what I knew about the area and the case. She asked if we could meet, and I agreed to meet her for coffee in—"

"You went on a date with my co-worker?" I could feel my blood pressure rising with each word he said.

"No, it wasn't a date, Laci. We discussed work. Her work."

"Why, Desio? Why did you agree to meet her?"

"I don't know. Because she asked me to? Because I didn't see anything wrong with it."

"You know she's only doing this because of me, right? Not only is she weaseling her way into my case, but she is also weaseling her way into my life. She is trying to take over both."

"That's a bit dramatic, don't you think, Laci?"

"I don't know, Desio—you tell me. You're the one who went on a date with her when you canceled ours. Well, you know what—you won't have to worry about canceling another one on me. I won't give you the satisfaction. I've got things to do—bye."

I hit the end button and screamed. The small group of seagulls to my left took flight, and one left a present on the picnic table in front of me. Served me right, I guess. My phone went off, and I automatically answered it.

"Major Duvall," I said.

"Laci. Will you—" Desio said, but there was no end to that sentence that remotely interested me. I quickly signed off again. Maybe I was being childish, but damnit, I thought we moved past all this and were on our way to a future.

My phone went off in my hand, but this time I checked. I didn't recognize the number, which meant I had to answer it.

"Major Duvall," I said.

"Major Duvall?" I knew this voice. I'd dreamed of this voice for years. "Major? Laci?"

"Asher?" I asked.

"Oh, good, you do remember me," he said.

"Holy shit, Asher. I never expected to be getting a call from you of all people. How are you?"

Lieutenant Colonel Asher Ellis. The only man outside of Desio to tempt me to do things I would never consider doing with anyone else. Not that we ever got that far. We deployed together ten years ago, and he let it be known when we left the theater he would be interested in pursuing things further. With him being Army, we never got the chance to find out if we were a hit or a miss. Asher was a tall strong nitro brew tea, and don't even think of adding sugar.

"I'm calling you because you were supposed to meet with two of my men this morning."

"Wait. You're the new CO for Westfall and Moffat?" I asked. "At Aberdeen?"

"Yeah, I just arrived last night. I'm sorry General

Fields had to be the bearer of bad news, but I needed to speak to the men first. When she told me the situation and who was in charge of the investigation she shocked the hell out of me. How long have you been back?"

We spent the next few minutes catching each other up on news and life occurrences. It was great to hear his voice again after all these years. While he didn't give me the same butterflies Antonio did, it was flattering that he was still very much interested in picking up where we left off.

"You still haven't married?" I asked.

"No, no," he said. "It was close about five years ago, but she called it off when I deployed. How about you? Anyone after Zach?"

"Nope," I said. I remembered my call with Antonio a matter of minutes ago and didn't lie. "I thought there was someone, but he wasn't quite there."

"Guy must be crazy," he said, and I laughed. "Do you want to get together for dinner, and we can discuss the case and anything else we can think of?"

I knew what he was getting at. "I think dinner would be nice," I said. "When and where?"

We agreed to meet that night at what used to be the Venetian Palace but was now called Venetian Italian Eatery. I would have to find a way to get there since Rev needed his car back.

****

The house was quiet when I got back. I set my bag on the table by the front door and tiptoed down the hallway to where it emptied into the dining and living rooms. Laying on the couch to the left with his mouth open and nothing coming out was Rev. His feet hung off one end by about a foot, and he was covered in a blanket. That wasn't the surprising part—the surprising part was Ryan lay splayed on top of Rev and was out like a light. I immediately brought my phone up so I could take a picture.

Movement in the backyard drew my attention, and I quietly pushed outside through the screen to where Sammie sat in the yard on a blanket with Ana asleep on her lap.

"Why are the twins home?" I asked Sammie in a quiet voice.

"The daycare had an emergency, and we were called to come get our kids as soon as possible. I swanny mine were there no more than thirty minutes when I had to turn around and come get them. The fire department was there when I got there, so I'm guessing it was something serious."

"How'd the interview go?" Cassy asked from the wicker chair on the patio.

"What interview? I got halfway there and General Fields calls to tell me I can't meet with the husbands because their new CO isn't here yet. Well, get this. Their new CO called me a little while later, and turns out we deployed together ten years ago. Long story short—Lieutenant Colonel Asher Ellis and I are going to dinner tonight to discuss the case."

"Yeah, somethin' tells me you leavin' a lot out," Cassy said.

"I agree with Cassy," Sammie piped in from the yard.

"Now, how the hell you figure that?" I asked.

"Why this dude callin' you instead of goin' through the right channels? Did you guys hook up while you was deployed?"

"No, we didn't hook up." I sniffed. "We weren't allowed to."

"But did you want to?" Sammie asked.

I thought my red face was plenty answer enough, and I was right. Cassy let out a holler, and Sammie giggled from the yard.

"Does Desio know 'bout him?" Cassy asked.

"No, which reminds me. Antonio had a date of his own with one Captain Wesley Hanscom."

"He did what now?" Cassy asked. "How you know?"

"He told me himself when I called him. Said they went to coffee so she could 'ask questions' about the investigation. Which is pure BS because he isn't even involved in the investigation."

"You sure it was a date?" Cassy asked.

"Yes, I'm sure. She asked, and he went."

"That don' mean nothin'. He could be just bein' polite."

"Now, wait just a damn minute. Why is it a date when Asher asks me, but when Wesley asks Desio, it isn't?"

"Because one is to dinner and one was just coffee," Sammie said.

"Please explain that logic to me," I said, "because I fail to see it."

"Coffee is whatchu do before you go on a date. You done skipped the pre-date and went right for the date."

I stared at Cassy with my mouth hanging open. That made absolutely no sense. "What?"

"Nowadays people go out for coffee to see if they want to continue to see each other," Sammie said.

"It's true," Rev said from the other side of the screen. He held Ryan in his right arm. "I had a coffee date once, and he never showed."

"Well, that sucks," Cassy said. I nodded in agreement. "At least have the decency to tell someone you ain' coming. Don't just not show up."

"Well, I disagree, and that's the only opinion I care about right now. It's just dinner with an old friend discussing work." And maybe a little bit more that I wasn't sharing right then. Besides, who even knew if he still felt the same—or if I did.

****

I rolled out of the European bus Rev borrowed from his mom for the evening and straightened my dress. Sammie made me take one of hers, but only because my good one was dirty. This was a black wrap dress, and no matter what I did I couldn't keep the top closed enough for my liking. I knew Asher would love it. Ugh. I tried to talk Sammie into something more casual, but she wouldn't hear of it.

The car door slammed behind me, and I turned to where Cassy, Sammie, Ana, Ryan, and Rev stood behind me. I tried to talk them out of coming, but they wouldn't listen. We were all in various states of dress.

Rev sported another cat shirt with jeans and combat boots, Sammie's casual dress matched Ana's, Cassy was in pink leopard print cropped pants and flats with a T-shirt, and Ryan rounded us out wearing shorts, a short-sleeved shirt, and clip-on tie. He was thoroughly adorable and currently attached to Rev's side.

Cassy called ahead and made reservations for them as soon as she weaseled out of me where I was meeting Asher. This was going to be interesting.

We got to the hostess stand, and I was told Asher wasn't there yet, but I insisted Cassy and crew go ahead and sit down. It was a short fight, but I ultimately won.

I stood to the side while others came in and claimed their seats. Some were given the little device to let them know when it was their turn to be seated. They usually went back outside to avoid cluttering up the hostess stand.

Ten minutes passed and still nothing from Asher. I was debating whether to join Cassy after she came for me the third time, but over her right shoulder I spotted a familiar face.

"What the hell did you do?" I asked Cassy.

"Now watchu mean?" she asked.

"Was this your idea?" I pointed to the front door, where Antonio stood staring at me.

"What the fu—why he here?"

"You mean this wasn't you?" I asked.

"Nuh-unh," she said.

Over Antonio's head, I caught sight of Asher. He was half a head taller than Antonio, and his eyes met mine. He squeezed through the small opening and approached me and Cassy, where he pulled me into a hug. In other circumstances, it would have been great to see Asher, but with Antonio, you know, right there, there wasn't enough sweet tea to keep the oncoming train away.

I was engulfed in a cologne-scented hug, and my head sat just under Asher's chin. I had to remind myself it was good to see him again. When he released me, I looked past him to where Antonio stood. He was obviously waiting for someone. I was caught between a rock and an Asher because I didn't know what to do.

Ultimately, politeness and twenty-plus years prevailed, and I excused myself from Asher for a second.

"What are you doing here, Antonio?" I asked.

"You tell me. I was told to meet a Lieutenant Colonel Ellis here to discuss an investigation. I wasn't given an option."

"Asher, why is Detective Desio here?" I wasn't going to beat around the bush on this. I wanted to know how Asher knew about him.

"I spoke with another OSI Agent, and she told me that Detective Desio here was helping with the investigation," he said.

"Would you care to confirm to me who it was you spoke to?" I asked, ohhh, but I knew.

"Some Captain who I'd swear was a woman but had a m—"

"Wesley. Captain Wesley Hanscom," I said.

"Yes," he snapped his fingers. "That's her."

I saw red. Again. I didn't know what she was hoping to accomplish, but if it took everything in me, this would be the last stop of her career.

"Could you please excuse me?"

I stepped around Asher and stalked to the hostess stand. I explained there had been a mix-up and we would need a table large enough to accommodate both parties at once. This created a flutter of hands and Italian too fast for me to understand. It didn't faze Desio. He stepped up behind me and asked to speak to the owner. When he came out, there was cheek kissing, Italian speaking, and hand gesturing, but it seemed all was forgiven.

We picked up Sammie and company on our way to a separate area. The table ran the length of the small room and reminded me of a restaurant I'd eaten at in Aviano. Menus were laid in front of us, and bottles of wine were uncorked before I knew what was happening. So much for a work dinner.

I was seated between Asher, at the end to my left, and Ana with Sammie on her other side on my right. At the other end of the table, to Sammie's right, was Antonio, and to his right was Cassy, followed by Ryan and Rev. Asher cast a wary glance at Rev, but I just smiled at him. Rev was a part of the family now; he must have known what I was thinking because he smiled really big.

Conversation flowed around me like water. Antonio was mostly quiet at his end of the table despite how much Cassy and Sammie tried to draw him into the conversation. I was constantly leaning against Asher's hand on the back of my chair, who didn't move when I touched it.

I felt a headache coming on that had nothing to do with the weather and everything to do with the testosterone coming off of Asher in waves—or it could have been his cologne. When I began to feel sympathy for Antonio, I remembered again his date with Wesley, and I felt my stomach tighten in response.

We were halfway through the appetizer when the owner came to speak to Antonio. I've known Antonio most of my life, and he was immediately upset. He got up and went with the owner, and I excused myself and followed him.

He made it to the hostess stand, and who should be there but Captain Hanscom.

"Why are you here?" I demanded from behind Antonio. He turned to me in surprise—he didn't know I was there.

"Why, *Major*, don't you look cute? I'm here at the invite of Lieutenant Colonel Ellis, did he not tell you? Why that silly goose."

"You're not welcome here, *Captain*," I said. "You are, of course, free to sit anywhere in the restaurant. Will your husband be joining you tonight?"

"Why, I don't believe that's your call, *Major*."

"What's going on?" Asher asked.

"I was ju—"

"I know you don't know any better, Asher," I interrupted her. "But *Captain* Hanscom is not a part of this investigation. She never has been. She never will be. She is not welcome at my table. I was informing her of this, and she tells me that you invited her. Now, is that the case here, Asher?"

I crossed my arms over my dress, but I felt my chest expand under the V in the dress, so I dropped them. I was so uncomfortable at the moment—for so many reasons.

"I was given the impression that she is assisting you," Asher said.

"Oh, really?" I asked. "Did you fail to understand a direct order from Colonel Waters, or were you hoping I wouldn't know about that?"

I placed my hand on my hips and impatiently tapped my foot. I sensed her desperation and rising temper. I wanted her to lash out because I wanted a reason to send her packing to another assignment.

"No, I didn't fail to understand him," she said.

"I'm sorry, no what?"

"No, *Major*." She gritted her teeth.

"Then you know what to do, Captain," I said.

She stared at me for another minute before she blinked and retreated to the front door. When she got there, she looked back one last time, but I hadn't moved. She pushed the door open and left the restaurant.

I needed a minute and excused myself to the bathroom. From there, I returned to our room. The end of the table opposite Asher was empty.

"Where's Antonio?" I asked.

"He ain' with you?" Cassy asked.

"I think he left with Captain Hanscom," Asher said.

"What makes you say that?" I asked.

"When you left for the bathroom, he went out the front door. He never came back here."

I collapsed in my seat and blew out a breath. I refused to cry over Antonio, but I wasn't ready to move on with dinner either. These were the moments when sheer willpower, twenty years of Air Force, and sweet tea were all I had to go on. I silently pulled myself together and finished the rest of my dinner, which suddenly tasted like sawdust.

Chapter Nine

The cicadas were outdoing themselves when Needles, Boo, and I pushed through the screen the next morning. It was early, and the house was quiet since I was the only one awake. I'd tossed and turned for the last hour and finally gave up and came downstairs. My heart was heavy, and I was sad and pissed at the same time.

The reason for all of the above was how I left things with Antonio last night. He never called, and I refused to call him once he left with Hanscom. This was the kick in the ass I needed to focus on my job and figure out this case before something else happened.

This morning, after Sammie dropped the kids off at daycare, we were going to Aberdeen to speak with Asher. I think having my girls with me would help boost my confidence and keep me on track. How were we getting there? Mr. Williams, Sammie's dad, dropped her car off while we were at dinner last night. He wanted to surprise her, and if her scream from the backseat didn't mean he hit the mark, then I didn't know what would.

I don't know how long I sat there before I heard Cassy. "Hey, Laci. Why you up so early?"

I met her in the kitchen, where she poured her first cup of coffee. I took a little bit for myself, even though I wasn't a coffee drinker, but with the fridge empty of sweet tea, I was desperate. Cassy added enough sugar and creamer to make a dessert out of her morning joe.

"No reason," I said.

She crossed her arms and gave me the same look Sammie gave the twins when she knew they were fibbing about something.

"You wanna run that by me again?"

"Fine, but where do I begin? Oh, I know—how about I start with the subordinate trying to steal my case out from under me? That reminds me—I need to update Colonel Waters. I really don't understand why she's so determined that *this* case be hers. Hmm, maybe I need to look into her relationship with the deceased as well as anyone else in the spouse's club. Something else to ask Waters. Anyway, there's that, and then there's where Antonio left with her last night—"

"Now, how you know they left together?" Cassy said.

"That's what Asher told me, and he has no reason to lie," I said.

"You takin' his word for it and don' think he has a reason to lie? How 'bout the fact that he know you and Desio's history. Who's to say he and Hanscom didn't come up with this scheme together?"

"Why would he do that?" I asked.

"Really? Are you that dumb?"

"Hey—" I interrupted her.

"Laci, you done told us you two flirted and considered a lot more ten years ago. How you know he hasn' forgotten that? You certainly haven't, so why would he?"

"I know. I know. You're right."

"Damn skippy, I'm right. Now, I may not have two

men at my beck and call, but I do know a thin—"

"I do not," I said.

"You don't what?" Sammie asked. She rounded the top of the landing with the twins sliding down the steps behind her. It was their favorite game.

"I do not have two men at my beck and call," I said.

"Well, maybe not beck and call, but that man you work with is down bad for you. But poor Desio, he's wound so tight he don't know which way is up. It's like my daddy used to say about our dog Roscoe, who had separation anxiety. We couldn't leave him for fear of him piddling in the house."

"I'm sorry, I fail to see how Antonio relates to your dog peeing on the furniture," I said. "And don't get me started on Asher getting down or whatever you said. Sometimes I think you guys do this stuff on purpose."

"Well, when a dog's got separation anxiety they piddle in the house in addition to signs of restlessness and depression. From what I saw of Detective Desio last night, that man is depressed. And seeing you with the other one got his feathers ruffled, and he didn't like that he was upset about it."

"Is it me, or did that just make a hell of a lot of sense?" I asked Cassy. "Then what am I supposed to do? I didn't ask for any of this."

"I would steer clear of the Army man to start with," Sammie said.

"I can't," I said. "I have to go through him to see Noah Westfall and Damian Moffat. General Fields already canceled on me once because he wasn't here—she's not going to let me speak to them without Asher's say so."

"Ain' there a way to question them in an official capacity without having to include all them? Ain' there an OSI 'cept for the Army?" Cassy asked.

I opened my mouth to argue, but I snapped it closed immediately. "Now that is not a bad idea. I don't know why I didn't think of it myself. They must be already holding their own investigation. While you guys get ready to go, I'll message Colonel Waters and see what he can tell me about the Army CID or Criminal Investigation Division. If I'm not mistaken, there's one at Aberdeen."

We went our separate ways, and I messaged Colonel Waters, since it was still early, to ask for some help. I didn't get into specifics, but I told him it would help me out if I could go through the CID instead of General Fields and the soldiers' commander.

****

With the twins dropped off, we cruised Pulaski Highway with Aberdeen Proving Ground, our final destination. The windows were down, and the music was up. It was Snoop Dogg today since Sammie got to pick—she continued to surprise me. No word from Colonel Waters yet, but I hoped he had something for me before we arrived.

I forgot Sammie wasn't with us when Rev, Cassy, and I came earlier in the week, so we took a few minutes to get her a guest pass. We were ready to make some much-needed progress. I did a quick search on my phone and located the office on Aberdeen for the CID. It was a relatively easy location to get to, and we would have made it fine if it weren't for the construction traffic on Aberdeen Boulevard. You would think with the workday still being thirty minutes from starting traffic would be low, but no, it was like rush hour on post. The Army were their own breed.

We were forced to detour into the PX parking lot along with the rest of the line of traffic. Once there, we parked and walked across the construction and Aberdeen Boulevard to the building we needed.

The CID office was located in the same building as the commander, except on a different floor. I really didn't want to see her because then I would have to explain how I circumvented her command, and I didn't think she'd care for that too much.

The hall was quiet outside the office, and when I pushed open the door, I put a little too much enthusiasm into it and it flew open and bounced off the wall inside.

"Damn, Laci." Cassy snorted.

The staff sergeant sitting at the desk jumped in his chair and swung around to confront us. He didn't look thrilled at our entrance.

"Sorry about that, Sergeant," I said. "Can you tell me who's in charge of this field office?"

"Who wants to know?" he asked.

Wow. "I'm Special Agent Major Laci Duvall, AFOSI, Sergeant Baker," I said.

"I'm going to need to see your ID," Baker said.

I arched one eyebrow and reached into my bag. I didn't take my eyes off of him. He looked unimpressed and bored. I placed my ID on the desk, ignoring his outstretched hand, and slid it over with the tip of my finger. I was used to the disbelief, but it pissed me off all the same.

He cleared his throat. "Yes, Major. Colonel Martin is the CO here. If you'll wait, I'll let them know you're here."

The girls and I browsed the pictures on the walls while we waited. I turned when I heard the door open, and Baker came out, followed by a woman in a colonel's uniform.

"Major Duvall, I'm Colonel Martin. I just got off the phone with Colonel Waters. Won't you join me?"

I gave the signal to the girls to stay in the outer office while I followed Colonel Martin inside and took my seat across the desk from her.

"Thank you for seeing me on short notice. Are you current on the case I'm investigating?" I asked.

"I have some information, but you can catch me up on what you know and how we can work together on this. I'll admit I fail to see why OSI is involved."

I raised my eyebrows at the subtle jab. "We're involved because we were at the scene, and no one from CID has reached out to me," I said. "Have you been conducting your own investigations?"

"We have, yes," she said. "The husband of the deceased arrived last night. I'm set to interview him shortly. I believe that's why you're here."

"Yes, ma'am, you're correct."

"Captain Hanscom is set to arrive within the hour. I don't understand why I am getting more than one of you to question one man."

I sucked my breath so hard I started coughing. It was either that or I'd scream.

"I'm sorry you've been led to believe there's more than one of us here for the interview. The fact of the matter is, it's just me who will be doing the interview for the OSI. Just like it is just me who is working the case."

"I don't understand why she is coming then."

"Well, ma'am, neither do I, but I will be assuring her if she arrives that she will not be participating."

Colonel Martin maintained eye contact for a few seconds longer. She knew there was more to this than I was saying. You didn't get to be in her position by being clueless, but one glance at my Cheshire smile and she knew not to push.

"Yes, well. Be back here in forty-five minutes, and we'll be ready for you."

I stood and grabbed my phone out of my bag in one move. Colonel Waters wasn't doing enough. It was time for me to take care of things.

"Give me a second, girls," I said. "If you want to go on to the car. I need to call someone."

"Uh-oh," Cassy said. "I know that ain' a happy tone. Come on, Sammie, let's go."

They left while I pressed Colonel Waters's number.

"What?" He always answered like I'd gotten him off the 13th hole at the Master's, but he didn't even play golf.

"Sir, I've had enough of Hanscom. What is it going to take to get her out of here?" I rehashed the dinner from last night in addition to the information that just landed in my lap.

"Major." I could practically hear the headache he had coming on. Well, he wasn't the only one.

"Sir, I have made it plain over and over again that she is not on this case. I'm not asking for your permission, but if she tries to step foot into this meeting, the MPs I'll be having on hand will remove her."

"Now, Major," he said.

"No, sir. I'm done being nice. Nothing I'm saying is having any impact. What is she saying to you when you tell her to leave it alone?"

"Well, as to that, Major, I've been discouraging her from bothering you more than I've ordered her to cease and desist. You are grown-ass women and need to act like it."

"Yes, sir. I understand. Well, sir, this grown-ass woman is taking things into her own hands from here on out. With all due respect, sir, you won't have to worry about me bothering you with this anymore."

"Keep me posted, Major," he said.

I was done playing nice. It was time for combat. On my way out, I went to the MPs office and asked for someone to be at the CID office at the time of the meeting. I told him I might need his help having someone removed. With this taken care of, I left to go meet Cassy and Sammie at the PX parking lot.

I wasn't prepared for what met me at the car. A trash truck sat blocking Sammie's car in the parking spot. Between the car in the back and the trash truck, there was no way Sammie was moving. But instead of sitting inside the car and waiting for him to move Sammie stood outside of the truck yelling at him.

"I swanny, if you don't get this dad-blamed thing out of here I'm going to show you what for." She kicked the truck tire and the driver looked at her from the driver's seat like she was crazy, and I admit I could see his point.

"Listen lady, I'm waiting fo—Are you with her?" he asked when he spotted me. Cassy was nowhere in sight. I nodded.

"Laci, I can't get him to move." *Kick.* "And I can't

move my car out until he moves his hunk of junk."
Kick. "He won't listen." *Kick.*

"Where's Cassy?" I asked.

"She went to get food at the place over yonder."
She followed that with another swift kick to his tires.

"Sammie, let's join Cassy, and maybe by the time
we're back, he'll be gone. Do you need coffee this
morning?"

"Yes." *Kick.* "We're not done here." She pointed at
the trash truck driver.

"It's okay," I said to the guy in the driver's seat. "I
would like it if you could move while we go get food."

"I was tryin' to tell her that, but then she went
nuts."

"Yes, well. Please see that we can get out when we
get back."

I dragged Sammie away from her car and the trash
truck over to the fast-food place next door. Cassy sat in
the corner of the dining area with a perfect view of the
parking lot we just left.

"You going to tell me why you left her out there?"
I asked.

"I was hungry, and she wouldn' leave." Cassy
shrugged. "I tried."

"Fine. I have to be back in thirty minutes for the
interview. Apparently, I'm on my own where Hanscom
is concerned. I'll explain in a second. Sammie, what do
you want with your coffee?"

She came with me, and I bought her breakfast as a
thank-you for driving. I'd give her gas money too, don't
worry. After we picked up our food, we joined Cassy at
the table, and I filled them in on my conversations with
Martin and Waters.

"Now don' that just beat all?"

"No kidding," I said.

"I swanny," Sammie said. "It's like he's afraid of her."

"I wish I knew why she was so intent on this case at the expense of all her others."

"Could be anything. Could be tryin' to impress Colonel Waters. Maybe she gotta honey she tryin' to impress. Hell, she could be tryin' to impress you."

"I highly doubt it's me she's trying to impress, but if she is, she's failing miserably. I have the MPs meeting me at the interview location, just in case. I don't know what it's going to take to get through to her. As for a honey—get this—she's pregnant."

"No way." "Really?" Cassy and Sammie said at the same time.

I nodded. "At least that's what her uniform tells me. I have yet to see it, but then it's probably still early. What do you think, Sammie?"

"The only way she's pregnant is if she's really early. I mean, she isn't even showing."

We finished up our food, and I walked with Cassy and Sammie to the car, which was now free of a trash truck. I gave them vague directions to get to the bay farther down Aberdeen Boulevard. I warned them they couldn't get into the restricted area but should turn left when they ran up against the fence. I'd let them know when I was ready to leave.

With pent-up energy needing to get out, I took the stairs to Colonel Martin's office at the end of the hallway instead of the elevator. My adrenaline was riding high, but I couldn't say if it was from the confrontation I was itching to have with Hanscom or if it was for the interview with Westfall.

I didn't know whether Waters tried to warn her off but based on our phone conversation from a bit ago, I was guessing he hadn't. This was further confirmed to me when I opened the door to the CID office and who was standing there arguing with an MP but Captain Hanscom.

"Well, hello, *Captain*. What can I do for you?" She jumped when I spoke to her and spun around to face me. She was surprised to find me there—that much was evident. I strolled into the room. Each step bringing me closer to her.

"Why M-Major…what are you doing here?" she asked.

"Now, that's funny. I was going to ask you the same thing, Captain. It couldn't be because you're planning to interview Major Westfall, could it? Because we both know this isn't your case."

She opened her mouth, and nothing came out. Her face was a mask of confusion and embarrassment. Suddenly, she pulled herself upright and squared her shoulders. I had almost reached her, and she took a step back in defense.

"I am here to interview him, Major, and there's nothing you can do to stop me."

"Now, Captain." My voice was as smooth as fresh tea going in a glass. "I've been nice to a fault while you've tried to weasel your way into my case. I know that Colonel Waters has discouraged you from helping, but I can see it's going to take more than that. *I'm* here to tell you that if you don't leave of your own free will, this nice MP will have you removed. If you fight him, he will have you arrested at my direction."

I didn't know if he could actually do that, but it sounded good. She didn't know if he could do it either, but the threat was enough for her bravery to fail. I was directly in front of her, and she turned her head away to avoid looking at me.

"Not only that," I said, "but if you don't leave, I will immediately begin the paperwork for your transfer to another location. In fact, I may do it anyway. Because you can't seem to listen to direct orders from anyone—let alone your CO."

Her head snapped around to where I stood about a foot in front of her. Out of the corner of my eye, the door to the colonel's office opened, and she stood in the doorway.

"Are you ready, Major Duvall?" Colonel Martin asked.

I held Hanscom's gaze for a heartbeat longer before I turned and walked to Colonel Martin's office. I didn't turn to make sure she left. Part of me hoped she'd stay.

Chapter Ten

Noah Westfall was a complete surprise. He was fifty if he was a day. I thought he would be as young as Jill, who was in her thirties. Of course, it could be the news that aged him.

Colonel Martin, Major Westfall, and I were the only ones in the meeting. Time would tell if it stayed that way. With the colonel and me on one side of the coffee table on the couch, Major Westfall looked defeated in an oversized chair on the other.

"First, let me say I'm so sorry for your loss, Major." Colonel Martin murmured her condolences beside me. I couldn't imagine what this man was going through.

"Major, did Mrs. Westfall give any indication that she felt threatened at home? Did she feel safe?" I asked.

"If she felt threatened, ma'am, she didn't mention it to me, but then she wouldn't. She was a strong, level-headed woman who took nothing from anyone. I always told her I wish half my men were as tough as she is."

"Major, is that how you would describe your wife's personality and character—strong and level-headed?" Colonel Martin asked.

"Yes, ma'am. A lot of people didn't like her directness. She could be off-putting to some. I know she's said and done some things that turned people away, but at home, she wasn't like that. She was nurturing and always wanted to have children, but we weren't fortunate enough to have any."

I remembered my interview with the neighbor who mentioned the terminated pregnancy. Did he not know, or did Mrs. Zimmer get it wrong?

"Did Mrs. Westfall have any hobbies?" I asked.

"Her only hobby was that spouse's club, ma'am."

He didn't sound like he liked it.

"What was her health like?" Colonel Martin asked.

"What do you mean?" he asked.

"Did she share any health concerns with you?" she asked.

"She's always had exceptional health. We had a scare a few years back with her gallbladder, but aside from the surgery to take it out, there were no issues, ma'am."

"Tell me what you liked about her most," I said.

He smiled and relaxed a bit. "I loved her smile and that she wouldn't take sh—anything from anyone. Sorry, ma'am. I liked how she constantly surprised me with thoughtful gifts. She had a knack with words and would write me poems and leave them hidden in the house. There won't be any more of those now." He reached for the box of tissues in the middle of the coffee table between us. I glanced at Colonel Martin, and her eyes met mine.

"Was there anything unusual or out of the ordinary that happened before your wife died?" I asked.

"To me? Or to her?"

"Oh. Well. I guess both," I said.

"Nothing unusual for her, I don't think. If there was, she didn't tell me. The unusual thing that happened to me would be the number of phone calls I received while deployed only to get there, and no one would be on the phone. I asked Jill to see if it was her, but she insisted it wasn't."

"Did many people know your phone number?" Colonel Martin asked.

"Anyone could find it, ma'am." He shrugged. "It wasn't a direct line—which made it difficult to get to and even more frustrating when I did get there and heard nothing but dead air."

"Can we go back to the spouse's club? Correct me if I'm reaching, but I sensed you didn't care for this hobby," I said.

"Ma'am, they were nothing but social climbers who benefitted off her work. None were willing to put in the time and depended on her to do everything."

"Was this something she reported back to you, or did you observe this?" Colonel Martin asked.

"Both," he said. "She would come home crying after a meeting where she was berated by other spouses and the sponsors. I witnessed it once, ma'am. They had a tent at the morale run last year—she was the only one who showed up to work the booth. Other spouses were there, but when they saw the booth, they acted surprised to see it."

"Were there any in particular who seemed to challenge her more than others?" I asked. "Did she get along with the other officers?"

"You're wanting me to mention Ruby Moffat, aren't you?" he asked.

"Major, it's up to you who you want to mention. I'm merely gathering information that will help us find out who did this," I said.

"Ma'am, I work with Damian Moffat, and I've known him for years. I've never had a problem with him or Ruby. Yes, Jill and Ruby didn't get along, but that's all there was to it. They just avoided each other."

"How did that work when you lived next door to each other?" I asked.

"We didn't mingle socially—there was no need for it. They had their friends, and we had ours. Our paths didn't cross unless they had to."

"What can you tell me about the billboard?" I figured someone needed to ask him. It may as well be the one who doesn't have to be on the same installation as he was.

"Ma'am. There's no proof Jill did that," he said.

"Was there actual proof against Ruby and Colonel Chandler?" I asked.

I could see he wasn't going to answer, which was answer in itself. He could easily see his wife as the victim, but not someone she bullied.

"Was it true they were going to take away her title and position?" I asked.

"I think I'm finished, Colonel." He stood up, and I didn't say anything while she walked him to the door.

"Well, Major, you certainly know how to clear a room," Colonel Martin said.

"I'm not one to beat around the bush, Colonel, when it's a murder investigation," I said. "He paints his wife as the victim, but I've spoken with several she's bullied."

"Oh?"

I spent the next twenty minutes recounting my conversation with the other officers. I also told her about the neighbor's slip about the pregnancy termination.

"Does he know?" she asked.

"I honestly don't know. Either he's a good actor, or he really has no clue—or Mrs. Zimmer doesn't. If I could just figure out which. Have you been able to speak with Ruby?"

"I have an interview with her this evening. Would you care to join me? I didn't mean to tease you. I admire your interviewing skills—they rival my own," she laughed.

I agreed to join her later that evening. I would just have to borrow Sammie's car or call Rev—oh boy.

I exited the office, met Sammie and Cassy, and we headed home. I recounted the interview and my take on it on the drive back to the house, and Sammie assured me I could take her car.

We reached home with plenty of time for me to get some office stuff done. I immersed myself in paperwork, and after lunch, I decided to take a nap. I went upstairs while Cassy and Sammie landed in the living room and set up the gaming system. They'd talked a lot of smack on the way home. Each one was convinced they'd wipe the floor with the other in bowling.

No sooner had I lay across the bed than Boo jumped up and curled into my side. The soft rumbling drew my hand down her back and then to her head, where I stroked her again. About the third time I felt her fur under my hand, I fell asleep.

*****

I woke with a start and grabbed my phone to check the time. *Whew.* I still had ninety minutes before I needed to leave. I got up and went to the closet to see if

Sammie was gone since my window sat at the front of the house. She was.

After a quick look in the mirror, I considered myself presentable, then left my room to see what was happening downstairs, if anything. Cassy was asleep on the couch and snoring like a freight train. Needles was curled up beside her and snored softly. When he heard me on the last step, he looked up then jumped down to meet me.

We pushed our way through the hanging screen, and I grabbed a tennis ball from the middle of the yard. We played about fifteen minutes before my phone ringing in the house caught my attention, and I went inside. Cassy was on my phone and held her finger up to me when I came in.

"Now what now?" Cassy asked. She held the phone out and put it on speaker.

"Y'all, I swanny, I know I can drive. These people really cream my corn. My daddy isn't gonna be happy when I tell him I was in another accident, let alone my car insurance."

"What happened?" I asked.

"Someone T-boned me in the parking lot of the kids' daycare. I hadn't even picked up the kids yet, thank God. I'm sorry, Laci, but this is going to take a little while. I know you needed my car to get to your interview."

"It's fine, Sammie. I'll call Rev and see if he's available."

"Okay. I'll be home as soon as I can."

We hung up, and I got Rev on the first try. He agreed to take me and would be there to pick me up and get me to Aberdeen in time for the interview.

"Wha's this interview for?" Cassy asked.

"I finally get to meet and speak with Ruby for the first time. You wanna come along?"

"Damn skippy," she said. "I'm curious about her. Wha's her husband like?"

"I'll let you know once I meet him, which I imagine will be when he shows up with her. You probably can't come into the interview, but hey, it gets you out of the house."

****

Rev picked us up a half hour later, and we were on the road right away. Cassy made me ride shotgun while she closed her eyes and held on in the back seat. He got us there in twenty minutes which for me would normally take thirty to thirty-five. Cassy and Rev still had their guest passes, so we were able to get on without being held up.

We were almost at the end of the duty day, so the parking had cleared enough, and we grabbed a spot in front of the building. I brought Rev in with me; no point making him wait in the car by himself. Besides, sometimes having him with me was useful. He and Cassy were arguing over the Os when we stepped out of the elevator on the third floor.

"Nuh-uh," Cassy said. "The greatest was Eddie Murray, and you know it."

"He was all right"—Rev shrugged—"but you gotta give it to The Ironman, Ripken. No one's going to touch his record, and that makes him the greatest."

I tuned them out and focused on putting one foot in front of the other. When I stepped inside Colonel Martin's office, my blood pressure shot through the roof.

"What the hell are you doing here, Captain?" It may have come out sharper than I intended, but man, this girl couldn't take a hint to save her life.

"I'm here for the interview," she said. "Didn't Colonel Ellis tell you I would be here?"

"I haven't seen or spoken with Asher, Captain, but you already know you are not welcome here. Do I need to call the MPs again?"

"She's here because I invited her," Asher said from the door.

"Asher, it's not your place to invite my subordinate," I said. "The captain and I have been through this already. She will not be attending this interview."

"Why?" he asked.

"Because it's my case, Asher. Because Colonel Waters put me in charge when he was forced to step aside."

"What's going on here?" Colonel Martin stepped out of her office and joined us in the reception area. "Why are you here?" She looked past me and presented her question to Asher.

"Damian Moffat is one of my men. I was informed by Major Westfall that you and Special Agent Duvall met with him this morning without informing me. General Fields and I agreed that I would be in attendance whenever my men were interviewed, so imagine my surprise when one is interviewed without my knowledge and a second one was on the books."

"I don't answer to you, Ellis," Colonel Martin said. "When time is of the essence, I don't worry about permission slips." I think I may have my very first girl crush. This woman kicked ass and took no prisoners—

just my style. "Major Duvall, are you ready?"

"We have to settle Captain Hanscom's presence, and then we'll be in," I said.

"Wasn't she uninvited once today already?" she asked.

Oh, yes, this was my kind of woman. "Yes, ma'am. That's what we were discussing."

Colonel Martin looked at Captain Hanscom. "You are not welcome. You're free to go."

"I disagree, ma'am," Hanscom said.

Ohhh noooo.

"Excuse me?" Colonel Martin said. Her voice was soft, but steel ran through it.

"I was invited to the interview by Colonel El—"

"It's fine, Captain," Asher said. "You're free to go. I apologize for wasting your time."

"Dayyuummm," Cassy whispered.

I knew how she felt, but I kept that to myself. I followed Wesley into the hallway. I wasn't finished yet.

"I expect to see no more of you on this case, Captain," I said.

She turned around, and if looks could kill, I would be dead. I didn't know what it would take to get through to her, but I hoped this was it. It took everything in me to keep from slamming the door shut behind her.

In light of the tension in the room, Cassy and Rev voted to stay in the outer office. Rev was pulling a deck of playing cards out of his back pocket when I left them.

Inside Colonel Martin's office was dead silence. Asher sat at one end of the table and Colonel Martin mirrored him on the opposite end. They pretended the other wasn't there. Hmmm.

"What time are we expecting Mrs. Moffat?" I asked.

"She should be here any minute," Colonel Martin said.

"Hey, Laci," Cassy stuck her head inside the conference room. "You sure that girl left the buildin'?" Cassy asked. "I hear more than one female in the hallway."

"Good point," I raced from the room, and sure enough, outside the door was Captain Hanscom facing a petite woman and a man. She was asking them a question. I interrupted her mid-sentence. "Lieutenant Colonel and Mrs. Moffat?" When their heads turned my way, I held out my hand. "Hi, we're meeting in Colonel Martin's office. If you'll follow me."

"Oh," Lt. Colonel Moffat said. "Captain Hanscom said she would be asking us questions."

"The captain is not a part of the investigation," I didn't even look at her. "We're in here."

They preceded me into the reception area, and I shut and locked the door to the hall behind me. Wesley had crossed the line, and now she would pay, but I had other things to do before I dealt with her.

Colonel Martin and Asher stood when I entered with Ruby and her husband, Damian. Introductions were made and water was offered, then we immediately got to work.

"Mrs. Moffat, what was your relationship with Jill like?" I started off the interview.

"Jill and I didn't get along," she said. "She dated Damian a long time ago, but when he moved on, she didn't. I think she wouldn't have cared for anyone he dated, let alone someone he married. I tried to be the bigger person and treat her how I treated everyone else, but it's like she intentionally went out of her way to point me out and embarrass me."

"Can you give an example?" Colonel Martin asked.

Jill was a petite woman. She was shorter than me by a couple inches but would have been taller than Sammie. She had brown hair which she wore in a messy bun on top of her head with fringe bangs swept to the side of her forehead. Her clothes were nondescript, and I got the feeling she was someone who tried to blend in but failed because she was pretty.

"The most recent was the billboard on Pulaski between Edgewood and Riverside," she said.

"Where did the picture come from that was used?" I asked.

"Henry Chandler's family and mine go back a long time. His sister was my babysitter when I was growing up. We were comfortable with each other, and Damian knew all about our friendship. Colonel Chandler was like a brother to me. The picture was from social media. The local newspaper covered Colonel Chandler's family reunion because they're a predominant family in Bel Air, where we're from. Jill used software to turn an innocent image into something awful. I have a copy of the original picture.

"Henry and his partner, Allan, left for California last week. You see, Major Duvall, Henry Chandler was gay. There was nothing between us, but no one knew except me and Damian."

"It was no one's business but his own," Damian said.

Damian was a short hot tea with a cinnamon stick.

His skin was the color of bronze, and his hair and eyes were black. He reminded me of Antonio, but I think Damian's heritage was Latino, not Italian. His voice was deep and pleasant and held authority. His was a voice you would listen to.

"Can you recount for us your actions the morning Mrs. Westfall was found?" Colonel Martin asked.

"Yes, ma'am. The spouse's club set up a booth alongside the ball field. I didn't want to be there when Jill was there, but Haylee and Miles talked me into it. I haven't been an active member since I lost the election to Jill. I decided with my pregnancy, I would take a break and focus on the baby instead of the club."

"Where were you before the body was found?" I asked.

"Haylee needed me to get something from her car with her. We talked while we walked to the car. Haylee has been a good friend through all of this. She's a good support. When we got there, she showed me what she needed to go to the tent. She said she had to make a quick call and she'd be right back. She told me I didn't need to wait for her, so I left with the stuff she wanted at the tent and didn't think anything else of it. I was at the tent maybe ten minutes when the scream came from the bathrooms. I thought it was kids playing because there were so many of them. It wasn't until Candice came and told me what happened that I knew Jill was dead."

"Can anyone vouch for your whereabouts leading up to the time the body was found?" Colonel Martin asked. "What about Mrs. Bishop?"

"She was with me up until the point she made a phone call. I didn't see where she went after that."

"What was it she wanted you to get from her car?" I asked. "Did you hear her on the phone at all?"

"I didn't stay long enough for the conversation, no," she said. "The box has our membership papers in it—that's what she wanted in the tent." She chewed on her lower lip and looked thoughtful.

"What's wrong?" I asked.

"It's nothing. It's just...we never brought those papers to events before. I think I remembered asking her why she needed them today of all days. It wasn't even membership sign-up time. Miles doubles as the Membership Chair, and when I came back to the tent, he asked me why I had them. When I told him Haylee told me to bring them over, he just shrugged and took them from me."

"After you brought the papers, you stayed in the tent?" I asked.

"Yes, Miles and I started talking and he was voicing frustrations with the club. It was always the same story with him. I think the only reason he ran for treasurer was so he could bug Jill."

Since that coincided with what he told me, I decided to let that slide.

"Do you think someone could be setting you up? Is there anyone you think would try and make it look like you did this?" Colonel Martin asked.

"I honestly don't know," Ruby said. "I thought I was friends with everyone in the club, but if someone did, then maybe we weren't."

"How well do you know the other board members?" I asked.

"Aside from Jill, I just met everyone when we moved here," she said. "They all seem to know each other, but with Damian's job, we were outside the realm of normal Army life."

"When was the last time you spoke to Jill in person?" I asked.

"Oh, wow," she said. She brought her hand up and covered her stomach. "I saw her at the Fourth of July event here at Aberdeen, but we didn't speak. Mmmm, maybe Easter?"

"Why then?" I asked.

"Easter egg hunt sponsored by the spouse's club. I asked her where to put something. She never answered me—pretended not to hear me."

"How well do you know Noah?" I asked.

"Not very well at all." She shrugged. "He hasn't spoken to me the few times I've seen him. I knew it was awkward that he worked with Damian, so I chose not to approach him."

"What can you tell me about the relationship with Noah and Jill?" I turned and asked Damian.

"Not any different than anyone else's. Being an Army spouse is tough. You're left on your own a lot and forced to be independent for long stretches of time. When the member comes back you have to adjust again. It's taxing on a marriage."

"Did Noah know about Jill terminating her pregnancy?" Out of the corner of my eye, I saw Colonel Martin's mouth fall open.

"Jill has never been pregnant," Damian said.

Ruby opened her mouth and closed it without saying anything.

"Ruby?" I asked.

"I don't know anything for certain," she said. She waved her hand at her husband. "Just wait, Damian. It's only been since I became pregnant that I recognized the signs in Jill. But how did you know?"

"I can't tell you," I said. "What signs did you recognize?"

"She was sick to her stomach a lot. At first, I thought it was a stomach bug. She got sick at the smell of chicken at our last event of the year in April. Then Haylee told me Jill told her how she missed her period."

Haylee's name was being brought up a lot. I think it would be a good idea to meet with her one-on-one. I glanced at Colonel Martin, and she looked at me. I'm pretty sure she was thinking the same thing I was.

"Why would Mrs. Bishop know this? Do you know?"

"From my own opinion, I think Jill liked to brag to someone, and Haylee just happened to be it. She did it a lot, according to Haylee."

"I think that's all my questions for now, Mrs. Moffat," Colonel Martin said. "How about you, Major Duvall?"

"I think so, too," I said.

Asher walked Damian and Ruby to the front door and left with them—which suited me just fine. I could talk to Colonel Martin better this way.

"Now, who is Haylee?" Colonel Martin asked.

"She's on the board for the spouse's club," I said. "I think it would be a good idea to speak to her away from everyone else."

"Good idea," Colonel Martin said. "Let me know if I can be of any help."

Chapter Eleven

"Why don't we swing by housing again before we leave," I said.

"Why?" Cassy asked.

"Because I'm nosey," I said.

"Knock yo' self out."

"Do you remember how to get there, Rev?" I asked.

He nodded, and we pulled out of the parking lot onto Aberdeen Boulevard. He drove at a sedate pace since I'd warned him numerous times how particular base security is with posted speed. Even though I didn't live on base anymore, I still found myself counting two Mississippi's at stop signs. There were just some things you never unlearn.

Once in Jill's neighborhood, I had Rev pull over at the beginning of the row. The houses were to our left and about fifty or so yards away. The sun had recently set, and the streetlights were on, but there was only one in working order for the whole block, which helped us hide.

"Now, tell me, what are we doin' here?" Cassy asked.

"There's something here," I said. "I can feel it. Give me a second."

I got out and pulled my OCP cap low on my forehead before I walked down the road in front of the car. The cicadas were out in force tonight and drowned any nearby noise. When I passed in front of Jill's house, I slowed my pace and strained my side-eye to see if I could see anything without turning my head. I kept the same position until I reached the end and turned to come back. Instead of staying on the road, I went to see if there was space along the backyards.

Some houses didn't have fences—oh boy. I held my breath and scurried down the property line for those houses, but the ones with fences I slowed down and took my time. I neared Haylee's backyard when, suddenly, the sliding glass door opened. Unfortunately, there wasn't a fence in her yard, but there was one in Jill's.

I didn't get a chance to run for it but dropped to the ground in an instant. Lucky for me, I dropped right on top of a pile of Rottweiler leftovers. *Shit*—literally. I thanked my lucky stars for my OCP shirt when my right elbow landed in it. I couldn't move for fear of drawing Haylee's attention to my position, but the smell was overpowering.

"It's okay, Ruby, I know. They have ways of weaseling information out of you. Yeah, that major is like a dog with a bone." I thought she was talking about me, but I couldn't be too sure. "What else did they want to know?"

I tried to breathe through my mouth, but that thought scared me for what I would inhale around the dog doo. Did flies come out at night?

"They asked about her pregnancy? How the hell did they know about that? What did you tell them? You told her I said what? Why did you bring me into it?"

Haylee was firing off questions faster than Ruby

could answer them, and from her tone, she was not pleased that her name had been dropped into the line of questioning. If she didn't like that, she really wasn't going to like me contacting her about interviewing her alone.

"It's fine, Ruby, I promise I'm not mad," she said. Then tell that to your tone. "Thanks for letting me know. I'll talk to you later."

The second she hung up, she dropped an f-bomb big enough to level the house. Now, I wondered why she would be that upset over Ruby casually mentioning her during the interview. It looked like I was right—there was something else going on here. This would have to wait, though, because Haylee stormed inside and slammed the door shut behind her.

I scrambled off the grass, completely forgetting the landing strip I was now sporting on the elbow of my shirt. I stuck to the fence the rest of the way and hung a left when I reached the end of the line.

Rev's car was to my right, and I made a run for it. I yanked open the door when I reached it and collapsed onto the front seat. I let out the breath I had been holding.

"What the hell is that smell?" Rev asked.

"Crap." I pulled my elbow off of the armrest on the door and stared in horror at the mark I left. "I'm so sorry, Rev!" I covered my face with my hands. "I'll clean it for you, I swear. Do you have a tissue or napkin?"

"Glove box. Don't you worry none, hon," he said. "This thing's seen worse than that. I had a friend puke all over the floor in the back when he got carsick. He never told me he had problems, so how was I to know?"

I yanked the glove box open, and a box of condoms fell out and landed on the floor with a thunk. I grabbed them and shoved them back in when a water bottle and napkins spilled out next. I grabbed the water off the floor and poured some onto the wad of napkins. I scrubbed on the armrest and got the mark off, but the smell stayed with us all the way home. Cassy rolled her window down to do what she could with the smell, but I couldn't touch mine because Rev warned me it wouldn't come back up if I did.

By the time we made it home, I was full up on Cassy's whining about the smell from the back seat. I paid Rev and gave him a hefty tip to use part of it to clean the car out. I apologized for the twentieth time and rolled out of the car and dragged my feet into the house.

I took my OCP shirt off at the front door and threw it directly into the washing machine, put in at least a gallon of soap and peroxide to see if it helped, then started it. I may still just throw it away.

Cassy must have gone straight to her room because she was nowhere to be found when I closed the front door behind me. Needles was in the kitchen, but I let him out so he could take one last turn around the backyard before bedtime.

I collapsed on the whicker loveseat on the patio and put my feet on the whicker and glass coffee table. From back there, you couldn't hear the cars whizzing by on Philadelphia Road.

"You out here?" Cassy asked.

"Yeah, I thought you went to bed already," I said.

"Nah, just needed to breathe in something that wasn' dog shit." She laughed.

"Sammie in bed already?"

"Looks like it."

I ran through the interview highlights for her. Recalling tones and subtle messages my ear caught but didn't know the importance of just yet.

"I think this Haylee gotta lot of explainin' to do," she said.

"Yeah, that isn't even half of it," I filled her in on what I learned in the backyard of Jill's house.

"Yeah, I betchu, she got somethin' to do with all this," Cassy said.

"I think so, too, but the trick is getting her to tell me," I said.

"Hear anything from Desio lately?" Cassy asked.

"Not since he left the Palace the other night when Hanscom did."

"I told you to ask him out. Have you done it?"

"How's Amaré now that you aren't there to harass him?" I asked.

She wasn't the only one who could avoid questions. She looked like she wanted to argue with me about changing the line of questioning, but she didn't.

"He fine," she said. "Said it's quiet around there now."

"Do you miss it yet?" I asked.

"Ehh, sometimes I do. Most times I don't. Wha's the story on Asher and that colonel you interviewed with?"

"You picked up on that too, huh?"

"Yeah, there was lots of undercurrents running through there tonight."

"I don't know that I know Asher enough to ask him about it."

"You could ask that man anythin', and he'd do it for you. Wha's it like being boujee with the boys?"

"Boo—what? What the hell does that mean?" I asked. "You're doing this on purpose, aren't you?"

"I'm jus messin' with you. Keeps you humble."

****

My office was quiet the next morning when I got there. Rev was busy, so I called a cab and it cost me twice as much as he did. Either I wasn't paying him enough, or he wasn't charging me enough; now to figure out which was the case.

I tiptoed past Colonel Waters's office and silently opened my door. If he didn't know I was there, then I wouldn't have to answer the questions he was dying to ask me.

I also hoped I wouldn't run into Hanscom. I didn't need the added headache of dealing with her today. It was past time to do something about her. If only the results of the interview last night would keep her out of my hair.

I logged onto my computer and sent some texts from my phone while it was booting up. Once I inserted my CAC card, I was ready to go. My first stop was the Defense Central Index of Investigations or DCII. I wanted to see whether Westfall or Moffat had a history I should know about.

My jaw dropped, and I let out a whistle when I got a hit on Major Noah Westfall. It looked like the reason he and Moffat were deployed together was out of necessity. Westfall received a General Officer Memorandum of Reprimand (GOMAR) two years ago, and it was written by Moffat. GOMARs are attached to your permanent record—which was not good for Noah.

123

This meant wherever he moved from Aberdeen, it would go with him. Yikes. It could also be why he wasn't promoted. His GOMAR stemmed from civilian criminal charges—possession of an illegal substance.

Further research revealed he'd had several Command Directive Investigations in his career. The most recent was for Equal Opportunity (EO) for sexual harassment of a junior officer under his command. The investigation was closed when the junior officer left the military.

Another incident was Westfall getting pulled over on base with a blood alcohol level of .11—well over the limit for Maryland.

Going back a little further in his record, I found a Letter of Reprimand. This one was for the generalized term, conduct unbecoming an officer, and wasn't attached to his permanent record. Once he left Bragg, it was removed.

It was a wonder this man was still in the Army at all. Not really knowing what the conduct was, I decided to look up Damian's records to see his assignment list and cross it with Westfall's, and sure enough, they were at Bragg at the same time. I reached for my phone in my bag and dialed up someone who might be able to help me get a few new questions answered. I waited for her to answer and fought against hanging up the phone. I needed to question Ruby without her husband present just to check my suspicion.

"Mrs. Waters? Kristen?"

"Yes, this is she. Is this Major Duvall?" she asked.

"It is, yes, ma'am. I have another favor to ask. Can you have Ruby meet me without her husband present?"

"Oooh, that's a tough ask, Major. Why do you

need her alone?"

"I'm not going to arrest her. For what it's worth, I don't believe she killed Jill, but there are some things I need to know that I'm not sure she'll answer if Damian is there with her."

"Hmm, let me see what I can do. I'll text you when I know something. Will that work?"

"Yes, ma'am, that will be fine. Thank y—"

The knocking on my door was immediately followed by it being pushed open. I looked up and Asher was standing in my doorway. I swallowed my groan and hoped he hadn't heard any of my conversation with Mrs. Waters. I hit end on my phone and turned toward him.

"Laci," he drew out my name in a way I used to find endearing but now sounded like nails on a chalkboard.

"Asher, what a surprise. What are you doing here?" I didn't even know he knew where I worked.

"I came to see how the investigation was going. What can you tell me?"

"I can't tell you anything, Asher, and you know it," I said.

"Awww, Laci, not even for old times?"

"No, Asher," I said.

"Well, then how about I take you to lunch?"

"It's not ti—" It was twenty until noon. Where had my morning gone? "Fine, Asher. Where do you want to go?"

"Pizza John's?" he asked.

"No." Too much Antonio there.

"Ummm, okay. There's a crab house around the corner from us. You want that instead?"

Sounded nice and close. "Perfect," I said.

I grabbed my ID from the computer, my bag from under my desk, then I ushered him out the door so I could lock it behind us. I couldn't chance someone coming in and snooping in my office. I didn't know if she was there today, but I wasn't going to push my luck.

"Why are you locking your door?" he asked.

"Keeping nosey people out," I said.

"Who's nos—Oh, hello there, Wesley," Asher said. "How are you today? We're going to lunch; would you care to join us?"

"Listen, Asher, I only have so much time. Either you and I go now so we can get back, or you and Hanscom go, and I'll fend for myself in my office."

"Now, Laci," Asher began.

Instead of waiting for his answer, I turned and let myself back into my office, then closed the door in Asher's face. The look of surprise as I closed it on him would be one I would always cherish. What on earth did I ever see in him?

I crossed the room to the windows that overlooked the courtyard. The bird feeder was still low, I forgot all about it. For now, I leaned my head against the window and felt the heat on the glass. I closed my eyes and thought of Antonio's eyes. I missed the man even when I was mad at him.

I returned to my desk and grabbed my bag before I changed my mind. I dialed the phone, and he picked up on the second ring.

"Detective Des—"

"Do you want to go to dinner with me?" I blurted out.

"Laci?"

"Yes, Antonio, it's me."

"I wish I could, Laci, but I'm knee-deep in—"

"It's fine," I said. "I'll talk to you later."

I hung up before he could reply—completely embarrassed. How did people do this type of thing? How did they date when both parties worked full-time jobs? My phone rang, and I knew without even looking who it was. I couldn't answer when my heart was in my throat, though.

Chapter Twelve

I poked my head out the door of my office, then quickly drew it back inside. There was no one in this building I wanted to see or talk to.

I received Kristen Waters's text with the meeting time for Ruby Moffat. We were meeting at the coffee shop in Golden Ring. Yes, the same one I've met everyone at. Kristen would bring her—this way Damian wouldn't know. I hated the subterfuge, but there were answers out there I needed badly.

Rev met me out front of the office, and once I fell into the passenger seat, I took a deep breath.

"Rough day, hon?" he asked.

I rubbed my temples with my fingertips. "Yeah, I've got a co-worker out for my job. An ex-could have been, interested in being a let's go, and now I get to meet a woman and ask her invasive questions. So, all in all, a great day."

"Wow, that's tough. What's an ex-coulda been?"

I huffed out a laugh. "A guy I used to know who is back in my life and wants to pick up where we left off ten years ago."

"This ain't the police detective, is it?"

"Nope. Someone else entirely—the tall one from dinner the other night."

"What happened to the detective?" he asked.

"I called and asked him out, and he said no."

"Just like that? He didn't give a reason?"

"He didn't need to give one, Rev. He said no. He tried to give me an excuse, but I didn't let him finish."

"How old are you, hon?" he asked.

Ouch. "Hey. I can get my feelings hurt at forty-three just as much as I could at twenty-three. Maybe even more so. There aren't so many men ringing my doorbell for a date these days. Not when I can take out their kneecaps from forty yards anyway."

"It sounds like you got two live ones right here in the present. What more could you want?"

"I want the one who doesn't want me to want me, and I want the one who wants me to not want me."

"Amen," he said.

I laughed at the ridiculous situation I found myself in, and then I cried. By the time we reached the coffee shop, my eyes were red and my nose was running.

"You ain't pregnant, are you?" he asked.

"Rev, you have to have sex to get pregnant, and I haven't had any of that since my ex-husband and I divorced over twenty years ago."

"Jesus, woman, no wonder you're pulling your hair out and crying all over the place. Go get yourself some. You want me to hang out and wait for you?"

My hysterical giggle escaped before I could stop it and before I asked him to wait for me. Who knew— maybe that's all I needed. If only it were that easy to "get myself some."

I pulled the door open and went inside. Kristen and Ruby were in the corner with the wall to their backs. They looked anxious, and Ruby looked like she hadn't slept in days.

"Hello, ladies. Thank you for meeting me again so

soon, Ruby," I said. "Are you staying for questioning, Mrs. Waters?"

"That's up to Ru—"

"Yes, please. I'd like her to stay. I think I already know what you want to ask me. It's about my relationship with Noah, isn't it?"

Mrs. Waters sucked in a breath, and her eyes widened.

"I'm not sure—I wasn't aware you two had one," I said. "I did find an LOR in his record this morning, and I know you were there at the same time."

"Just so you know—it's not what you think. I didn't have an affair with Noah. He—he was my dealer."

"I'm sorry—your what?" I asked.

"My dealer," Ruby said. "Up until a year or so ago, I was a drug user. Anything and everything I could find, I did. It almost wrecked my marriage. Damian came to me for a divorce, and that was the wake-up call I needed."

"How is Noah allowed in the Army if he's a dealer?" I asked.

"It's not general knowledge, Major," she said. "Obviously."

"How did Jill know about you and Noah?" I asked.

Ruby hung her head for a second before looking at me. "I wish I knew. She figured out what he was doing and turned him into his CO. That's why he was issued the GOMAR. We thought once we left Bragg, it would be over, and it was until we came here. I couldn't believe it when I saw her the first time. She threatened me and tried to blackmail me, and there wasn't a damn thing I could do about it. Yes, I wanted to kill her. In the rhetorical sense—not the literal."

"Did you do anything about the blackmail?" I asked.

"No, but I reminded her that it wouldn't go well for her if word got out that her husband was a drug dealer. How would that make her look? That's all it took, really, because she's a reflection of the military as a whole. Where image is everything."

"How did this affect their relationship?"

"It was around that time that she terminated her first pregnancy," Ruby said.

"Her first? You mean there's been more than one?" I asked.

Ruby nodded. "I think she was pregnant when she died. I have no proof, but something Haylee said made me consider it."

"What is Haylee's relationship to you and to Jill?"

"She's the buffer between us."

"How so? Can you give me an example?" I asked.

"Jill told people I was bashing the spouse's club to anyone who would listen. She had the vice president and more than half the club on her side. There was nothing I could do or say. I went to Haylee as a last resort, and she volunteered to speak to Jill for me."

"Did it help any?" I asked.

"I—" Ruby stopped. "You know, I don't know. Now that I think about it, nothing seemed to make her hate me less. If anything, she hated me more."

Mrs. Waters caught my eye and gave a slight shake of her head. I respected her wishes and moved on. She may have something for me later.

"Back to Jill and Noah's relationship. Did Noah know about the pregnancies?"

"I honestly don't know," Ruby said. "We're not that close."

My phone rang in my purse, and I reached down and shut it off, but not before I saw Asher was calling me. Again. The man was persistent, I'd give him that. Thinking about him even for a second threw me off stride, and I stared at Ruby while thoughts raced through my brain. I shook my head to clear it.

"Does anyone else know about the relationship you had with Noah?" I asked.

"I didn't tell anyone," Ruby said. "I don't know if they did or not. It was a huge mistake on my part and one I live with every day."

"Can you think of someone who would want to hurt Jill?" I asked.

"Jill would have done well in the Army—she strategized like a soldier. She picked her friends based on what they could do for her."

"Did she tell you this, or is this observation?"

"This is what Haylee and I deduced," Ruby said. "Would you agree, Kristen? Based on your observation?"

Mrs. Waters gave us the deer in the headlights look but didn't reply.

"I think I heard she was being removed from her position as president. Do you know if that's true?"

Ruby looked surprised. "If that's the truth, then it's news to me. You would have to take that position away from her cold d— Well, she wouldn't give it up easily."

Mrs. Waters, Ruby, and I parted ways, and I went outside to see if I could find Rev. He was leaning against his car, talking on the phone.

"You got another job?" I asked.

"Yeah, you ready to go?"

We got in, and he peeled out of the parking lot like we were going to a fire. I knew to expect it, but it didn't mean I was prepared. My head hit the headrest, and I swore my heart stayed in the parking lot.

"Did you find out what you needed?" he asked.

"She confirmed my suspicion, but it doesn't lead me to figuring out who did this any more than I knew already."

"Are your cases always this tricky?"

"Mmmm, there's usually some element of mystery about them. I like puzzles, and to me, that's what my job is—figuring out the puzzle. Some have a lot of pieces, and some have few, and some have pieces missing until I find it under the proverbial table."

We made it home in under fifteen neck-breaking minutes. When Rev pulled into the spot out front of my house, he slammed on the brakes, and my hand shot to the dash to keep myself from getting a concussion. Maybe I should carry a pillow with me to cushion the blow to the head.

"Why don't you start a tab for me, and I'll pay you on payday? Can we do that?"

"Sure, hon. Whatever works for you."

"If you need it sooner, then by all means, let me know, and I'll pay right away."

He laid rubber on the road after I waved him off. Literally. I could see the tread marks from my parking spot to the pull-out on Route 7. Before I took two steps toward my house, a door opened on a sports car two spots over. Out of the corner of my eye, I saw a man get out, and he looked familiar. I gave him my full attention and groaned. This was all I needed—Asher—at my house.

"You don't give up, do you, Asher?" I asked.

"Not when there's something I want, no." His smile didn't quite meet his eyes. "And you're what I want, Laci."

Asher reached me by then, and I looked up into eyes the color of the ocean. It would be so easy if I was attracted to him instead of Antonio. But then I remembered Antonio's declaration of love, and I knew I would never be interested in the guy in front of me. Before I could tell him that, my front door opened behind me, and Cassy stuck her head outside.

"It's about damn time you got here," she said. "Where's Rev? I need a ride."

"He had another call and had to go," I said. "Where's Sammie?"

I turned to the house and gave my attention to Cassy. I didn't want Asher here, so maybe if I ignored him, he'd go away.

"Do you need a ride somewhere?" he asked. He refused to be ignored. "I can take you where you need to go."

"Asher, we're fine. We got this."

"Speak for yourself, Laci. I got to be at a job interview in twenty minutes. I was counting on Rev's driving to get me there. Can you drive fast?" Cassy asked Asher.

"As fast as I need to," he said. "Laci can come with us."

I opened my mouth to decline, but Cassy accepted his offer for both of us.

"Fine," I said. "Let's go. Where are we going anyway?"

"I'll give you directions." She folded herself practically in half and fell ass-first into the bucket seats in the back. "We goin' to the city."

"What's the name of the place?" I asked.

"I can' remember," she said. She avoided looking at me despite me turning around in the front seat to look at her.

"So, you're going to a job interview at a place you don't know the name of but know the directions to? Have you been there before?"

"Yes, I been there before," she said.

Her tone was rising, so I decided to stop asking her questions, but my mind didn't turn off as easily. Before I realized it, we were at the entrance to the Fort McHenry Tunnel. How the hell had we gotten here so fast? Where were we going? Then I knew. I swung around so fast I gave myself whiplash.

"You got a job with Zucca, didn't you?" I asked.

"What is Zucca?" Asher asked. "Pumpkin?"

"How do you know what zucca means?" I asked.

"Four years of Italian in college and three years stationed at Aviano," he said.

"When were you at Aviano?" I asked.

"Right before I came here."

"Zucca is an Italian mob boss who owns the Purple Pelican strip club. Please tell me you're not dancing, Cassy."

"Hell no, I ain' dancin'. I don' even know if I got the job yet. It's for a bouncer. The last one up and left, and Luca been filling in. I seen the advertisement last week on social media. Pumpkin Spice been tryin to get cops to make his place look legit."

"Pumpkin Spice?" I snorted.

She grinned really big. "I shocked him the first time I called him that, but once Luca stopped laughin', he started callin' him that too."

"How did I not know you've been talking to Zucca so much?"

"You been busy," she said. She turned her eyes to Asher in case I missed her meaning.

"Does Amaré know you're interviewing here?" I asked.

"Oh, no," she said. "An' he ain' gonna. You say anythin' and paybacks will be hell."

"How does this fit in with law school?" I asked.

I noticed Asher was keeping one ear on the conversation as he maneuvered his way through Baltimore City traffic. I admired his hands on the steering wheel and the way he handled the sports car.

"I gotta have something to pay for bills and tuition. Momma's money only went so far."

"Which school did you pick?" I asked.

"I haven' yet," she said. "This here the turn. Thanks for taking me. You guys wanna hang out until I get back? Shouldn' be very long. I'm not starting today."

"Sure, we'll wait," I said.

I got out of my seat, helped Cassy out, then watched her until she disappeared behind the door of the club. I saw too much of this place in the last month and didn't see how Cassy could return so soon. Of course, it wasn't her ex-husband who frequented the place either—I guessed that would make a difference.

"Tell me the story of how you two met," Asher said when I got back in the car. He turned his body toward me and leaned forward over the center console.

I gave him the abridged version, touching on Zach's death and how Sammie came to live with me. I didn't mention Antonio, but Asher knew about him. The Purple Pelican was behind us, and I shifted in my seat to look out the back window. When I turned back to the front, I ran into Asher's lips when he leaned over and kissed me. I wondered how long it would take him before he made his move.

We'd never made it past this stage ten years ago, and I admit I was having a hard time remembering why we didn't. He held my face in his hands, and I forgot to breathe. I'd forgotten what it was like to kiss him, and he was just as thorough now as he was then and made sure to hit every corner.

When reality returned, I pulled away from his lips and hands. Which was harder than I thought it would be. I opened my eyes and fell into the ocean blinking across from me. He went to pull me back in again, but I backed up in my seat.

"I could easily do that again, Ash, and you know it," I said.

"You taste just like I remember." He was still leaning across the console, and I wasn't able to look away. "I'm not going to give up, just so you know. When we're living this close, I would be a fool to let you go again."

Before I could answer, Cassy knocked on my window, and I jumped in my seat.

"How'd it go?" I got out to let her in.

"I got the job if I want it," she said.

"You don't sound as sure now as you did when we drove in. What happened?"

"I think it's just seein' the place again and

remembering all that happened," she said. "I got time to figure it out. He givin' me a week to let him know."

"Are there any other jobs out there you're interviewing for?" Asher asked.

"Not yet, but then I just started," she said.

We rode back to my house in silence. When I was with Asher like this, it was hard to remember why I was saying no.

Chapter Thirteen

My phone woke me up out of a dead sleep the next morning. Who the hell was calling me this early. It was four in the morning.

"Yesh?" My eyes were too blurry and unfocused to see who was there—not to mention my brain hadn't even caught up with my mouth yet.

"Ham and cheese omelet, Major," Colonel Waters roared across the airwaves.

"Yesh, sir?" Well, that was a new one. My mind peeled back the layers of fog and tried to make sense of him calling me. "Wash wrong, sir?"

"Major Duvall, Ruby Moffat is currently en route to Franklin Square. I need you there ASAP."

"What's happened, sir?" I jumped out of bed and ran to the closet. I narrowly avoided falling over Boo when I scared her off her spot on the pillow beside my head.

"Overdose of sleeping pills. Her husband is beside himself. No one believes she would overdose—something's fishy. I told him you would be there."

"Yes, sir. On my way, sir."

I had one leg in a pair of running shorts when I hung up, and my momentum carried me to the front door, where Sammie left the keys. In desperation, Mr. Williams, Sammie's dad, had agreed to let us borrow his car until one of ours was fixed. I could imagine what his yard looked like right now—a graveyard of chrome and rust.

I chucked my sweet tea bottle into the cup holder—thankful I'd paused on my way through and grabbed one from the fridge. With no time for a note, I'd text the girls from the hospital.

There was virtually no traffic this time of the morning, and I pulled into the closest spot in under ten minutes. Thankfully, I was only a few rows from the entrance and jogged through the front door, where the woman at the front desk jumped when I appeared.

"Hi there, I'm here for Lieutenant Colonel Moffat. Did he leave word for me?" I asked.

"Not with me, he didn't," she said. "Let me see what I can find out." She lifted the phone and placed a call.

While she waited for someone to pick up, I retreated to the chairs in the waiting room. Left alone with my thoughts, I realized this was the second time in a month someone I met at the coffee shop later met a tragedy. Last month, it was my co-worker's ex-wife who was killed. I prayed that Ruby would be spared the same fate.

I couldn't sit still, so I jumped up and paced back and forth for about eight minutes when the receptionist returned. Wait, when had she left? Before the doors shut behind her, Lt. Colonel Moffat pushed his way through them, caught my eye, and signaled for me to come with him.

"Good morning, Colonel Moffat, sir. What's happened?" I asked.

"Ruby began taking a prescription sleep aid shortly after we moved here when all these events happened with Jill," he said. "She's been weaning herself off with the help of her doctor since she became pregnant, though. Last night, she took some immediately after dinner. She doesn't usually take them so early in the evening, but she was anxious about something and wouldn't tell me. In a matter of minutes, she was gurgling, and her lips were blue. I knew right away what it was and called 911. We were recently briefed on fentanyl and other drugs and the side effects of overdoses. That's the only reason I knew what it was."

"You don't believe she did this willingly?" I asked.

"No, she would never do anything to hurt the baby. Not when we've struggled so much to get pregnant. I don't know what's going to happen to the baby after this, though."

We reached the small room where Ruby was lying on a bed under sheets and blankets. She was hooked up to several machines, and they beeped in the background.

"How far along is she?" I asked.

"Three months. She just cleared the first trimester." He went to the other side of Ruby and picked up her hand and held it. "Her pregnancy has been relatively easy so far. No morning sickness to speak of, and still the same amount of energy she's always had."

"Any funny cravings yet?" I was trying to take his mind off of the thought of losing the baby.

"Not yet, no." His smile didn't reach his eyes. "She's looking forward to sending me to Groovs in the middle of the night or the commissary for random items when the time comes. We joke about it. I don't know that we'll joke about it again, though."

"What do you think happened, sir?" I asked.

"I wish I knew," he said.

"How often does Ruby take the medicine for anxiety?"

"She only takes it as needed," Lt. Colonel Moffat said.

"So, it could have been there for a while. Have you had any company to your house lately?" I asked.

"Just the neighbors stopping by—which isn't anything out of the ordinary. It's something they do all the time. In fact, Mrs. Zimmer stopped in last night, and Haylee was at the house when I got home from work yesterday."

"How close are Haylee and Ruby?" I asked. Haylee's name had been recurring more and more, and I'll admit I didn't believe in coincidences.

"They're as close as they can be for this being their first assignment together. They met through the spouse's club."

"I'm gathering you don't have a soft spot for the spouse's club, sir," I said.

"Just a bunch of gossips and social climbers," Damian said. "They all pretend to care about each other, but when it comes down to it, they'd backstab their own mother if it meant getting attention."

"What do the base commander's and co-commander's spouses have to say about Jill's death?"

"They count it a tragedy and seemed shaken with the news that something like this could happen in our little neck of the woods. They don't speak to me directly due to Ruby's position, and that doesn't do much in my respect for them. I've put in for a special assignment to get out of here as soon as possible."

"Will they let you leave, sir?"

"Ruby hasn't been named a suspect. I imagine this isn't going to get us any sympathy, either. Others will view it as an admission of guilt, but I know she would never do something like this. I just need her to wake up and tell me she wouldn't."

"What do you need from me, sir?" I asked.

"I need you and Colonel Martin to find out who killed Jill so we can get the hell out of here."

"Does Colonel Martin know I'm here?" I asked.

"Yes. She couldn't make it this morning and suggested I call you. I didn't have your number, but Kristen Waters was the next best thing."

"What diagnosis do the doctors have for Ruby?"

"They think we got here in time for her to make a full recovery," he said.

"Can I make a suggestion, sir?" I asked. He nodded. "I would suggest not letting anyone know you're here, but if word does leak, I would keep people out—don't let anyone in to visit."

"You think that whoever did this will take a chance and try again?"

"I'd rather be safe and cover all the bases. It won't hurt to keep people away, especially with a baby to think about. Do you have the container the pills she took were in?"

"I gave them to the EMT when he asked for it."

"Did they pass it alo—"

The door opened behind Lt. Colonel Moffat, and a man in scrubs and a stethoscope came in. When he spoke, he confirmed my impression of a warm tea, milk added first, but no sugar kind of guy with a great bedside manner.

"Oh, hello," the doctor said. "I didn't realize you

had company. I came to see how Mrs. Moffat was doing."

"Doctor…?" I asked.

"I'm Dr. Tangen." He reached over, and I shook his hand and introduced myself.

"Dr. Tangen, do you have the pill bottle that was given to the EMT at Mrs. Moffat's house?" I asked.

"Oh, you know what, I don't. I can look in the system who brought her in and then contact their unit to find out where the bottle went. I'll do that once I finish with Mrs. Moffat here."

Dr. Tangen went about his duties in silence, and I stepped away from Ruby for him to get a better look. Lt. Colonel Moffat didn't leave her side.

"How is the baby looking?" I asked. Damian's head whipped up, and he stared at the doctor. The hope in his eyes was recognizable and heartbreaking.

"It's still too early to tell," Dr. Tangen said. "We're monitoring her 24/7 to make sure she has a chance to pull through."

"The baby is a girl?" Lt. Colonel Moffat asked.

"Oh, yes," Dr. Tangen said. "Very strong heartbeat when she came in. You brought her in early enough that she stands a chance at recovery. Well, I'll see what I can find on the EMT. I'll be back as soon as I can."

The door closed behind the doctor, and I could tell by Lt. Colonel Moffat's stunned face that up until now, he hadn't known they were having a girl.

"You didn't know, did you?" I asked.

He gripped Ruby's hand tight and shook his head. I decided to give him a few minutes and left the room to find Dr. Tangen. One glance at the nurse's station revealed that he wasn't there. Instead of hunting him down, I went through the double doors to the lobby so I could take a breather. I needed to text Cassy and Sammie and let them know where I was.

I stepped into the morning sunshine, pulled out my phone to message the girls, and inhaled the humid air. There was something about the smell of humidity that turned the morning beautiful. It was something I would never grow tired of. Being stationed in California and Colorado was torture—not just to my hair but to my soul. You can take the girl out of the humidity, but you can't take the humidity out of the girl.

After a little back and forth with Cassy and Sammie, they decided to try Rev to get the kids to daycare. I hated that I had the car, but I didn't have a choice. I would do my best to get it back to her before she needed to pick them up at the end of the day.

I hit the cafeteria on my way back to Ruby's room and grabbed a sweet tea and added another four packets of sugar. When I reached her room a few minutes later, I noticed Dr. Tangen leaving a room two doors down. I quickly stepped over so I could speak to him before I lost him again.

"Dr. Tangen?" I asked.

"Oh, hello," he said. "You're with Mrs. Moffat, right?"

"Yes, did you have any luck with the medicine bottle?"

"Oh, I'm afraid the only luck I had was bad luck," he said. "It seems the EMT left without turning it over to the emergency room team. We're trying to find him now."

"Do you know his name?" I asked.

"I do not," he said. "I can put in a request to the IT

team, and they can give it to me, but it will be a few days."

"Could you do that and then call me? I think it's important that we find the bottle sooner rather than later." I handed him a card from behind my phone, a place I kept them in case of emergency.

"Okay, I'll see what I can do."

"Were you the one who greeted Mrs. Moffat and the EMT team?"

"Yes," Dr. Tangen said. "Really, we're doing everything we can. I'll let you know when I know something."

He stepped away from the nurse's station, and I was left with no choice but to go back to Ruby's room. I tapped on the door, and Lt. Colonel Moffat pulled it open from inside. Once inside, I briefed him on the information I'd gathered, and with nothing left to do but wait, I grabbed a chair and placed it outside the door until further notice.

I grabbed my notebook from my bag and jotted down a few notes—gathering my thoughts on Ruby and who she saw leading up to the overdose. I didn't think it was a coincidence that Haylee was at her house the day she overdosed. In my opinion, she was too helpful in her dealings between Jill and Ruby.

What would she gain if Ruby was out of the way? What was her history like with Jill? She told Miles something different than she told me. I think it would be a good idea to speak to her, but would she willingly meet me?

I reached for my phone and texted the one person who could help me. My phone rang a few minutes later without a reply to my text.

"You want me to do what?" Kristen Waters asked.

"I need to meet with Haylee alone. Do you think you could do that?"

"No offense, Major, but I'm not sure talking to you is such a good idea."

"*Ouch.* I mean, I understand. I can meet wherever she wants and whenever she wants, but the sooner, the better. I need to get to her before news of Ruby gets out." I knew she was thinking about my history with the coffee shop visitors.

"I'll see what I can do, Laci, but no promises. I'm not forcing her."

"Thank you, Kristen. I appreciate it. You can just text me."

Fifteen minutes later and I had a time and place to meet Haylee. Tomorrow, noon, the fast-food joint in Riverside. I would need to be on my game if I wanted to get anything from her. She didn't need to know she was my number one suspect.

****

I made it home in time to turn the car over to Sammie for her to get the twins from daycare. I collapsed on the couch and put my feet up and closed my eyes. Needles dropped his tennis ball in my lap, but I was already too far gone to be of any use to him. I felt him snag it before he ran through the hanging screen to the outside. That was the last thing I knew before I fell asleep.

A warm body on my lap drew my attention from the dream I was having about Asher. Where the hell did that image of him come from? I opened my eyes and peered into beautiful blue eyes above a rosebud mouth with a thumb stuck in it. I smiled down at Ana and leaned forward and kissed her on top of her head. She lay back against me, and I turned on the TV to cartoons.

I heard Sammie upstairs in their room and Ryan babbling about carrots in the kitchen. He stood at the open door of the fridge and reached into the crisper drawer where we kept his and Ana's snacks. Instead of the carrots he was looking for, he found the container of blackberries and wrenched it open. Before I could get over there, he'd already gotten it open, and the few he managed to keep in the container and not on the floor he stuffed in his mouth. The juice dribbled down his chin and landed with a splat on the floor.

I took the container from him and lifted him and it into his chair at the dining room table. He didn't scream, which was progress for him. If anyone but Sammie or Rev picked him up, he let us know how much he hated it by screaming. While I hunted for blackberries, Ana was in the fridge looking for fruit of her own. I grabbed the grapes, washed them, and put them in front of her next to Ryan at the table. They were immediately drawn into their cartoons, and I cleaned up the blackberry juice off the floor.

"Did Ryan do it again?" Sammie asked, coming down the stairs.

"It's okay," I said.

"I didn't want to wake you when we got home. How'd it go today?"

I filled her in on everything as we stood around the kitchen. "Where's Cassy?" I asked.

"Amaré called and asked her to go with him somewhere. He came and got her since her car is broke. I swanny we don't have any luck with cars, do we? Daddy says he'll get to yours just as soon as he can.

Momma's brother is demanding his time for some project or other, and my Uncle Randy doesn't understand that Daddy has other things he has to do besides help him. Daddy's too nice to say no, and if he did try, Momma would guilt him into it. It's too much drama for me, so I just stay the heck away."

"I can get my car to the shop if it's too much for your dad, Sammie. I only asked him because he wasn't busy at the time."

"Oh, I know that, and so does he, but he wants to. He just wasn't planning on Uncle Randy."

"Okay, if it gets too much, let me know. How are things with Janice and Floyd?"

"Oh, it's okay." She looked toward the twins at the table. "She's been asking about taking the twins overnight again. I know I can only put her off for so long before I have to give in."

"What do the twins think of them?"

"Oh, they love Nanna and Papa, which is what they want to be called." Sammie shrugged.

Before I could say anything else, Cassy came through the front door. I heard her bag hit the table and her shoes come off on the tile floor.

"Hey, Cassy, how'd it go with Amaré? What'd he want to show you?"

"Damn fool wanted to show me some drone he got. He 'bout lost it to his neighbor's dog, though. We had to pry it from him, which he took to mean we was playin', which really got the tug-o-war started." Cassy started laughing, and it was the loud one I loved so much.

Hmmmm. "Cass, do you think Amaré and his drone would help us out if we asked? I just had an idea."

"Uh-oh, wha's your idea?"

I laid out my plan to go back to Jill and Ruby's neighborhood and do some snooping, and how the drone would help us.

"Sammie, do you want to call Janice and Floyd to give them their opportunity, or do you want to stay here with the kiddos?"

"No way are y'all leaving me out of this. I'll give them a holler and tell them the good news."

The only thing left to do was wait for tonight and finalize my internal plan. I rubbed my hands together in anticipation.

Chapter Fourteen

With Amaré among our numbers tonight, we didn't need Rev to drive. This was probably for the best—we didn't need the extra attention a seven-foot giant would give us. The guys at the gate didn't spare us a second glance, and we got Amaré signed onto base in short order. I guessed they were used to all sorts, and that included a group all dressed in black coming onto base, excuse me—*post*, on a weeknight.

Cassy directed Amaré to housing and, specifically, the road where the Westfalls and Moffats lived. The fact that Haylee also lived on the street was an added bonus.

"With Ruby and Colonel Moffat in the hospital, I'm not sure what to expect by way of neighbors tonight. There are some on the street I don't know—for instance, I don't know who lives on the top and bottom of the street."

"Does it matter?" Cassy asked.

"Not really," I said. "I'm just curious."

"What's the order that you do know?" Amaré asked.

"Mystery neighbor one, the Zimmers, the Westfalls, the Moffats, the Bishops, mystery neighbor two, and mystery neighbor three. The only two without a fence are mystery neighbor three and the Bishops. I'm not sure if that will be a help or a hindrance."

We parked two streets over from the one we were watching and retraced our steps through the grassy area between the roads. We began on the farthest end from Jill's house, down by mystery neighbor three.

"Amaré, are you all set to run the drone?" We did a test run at my house so I could see the noise level, radius, and viewing quality.

"Yes, ma'am. We're all set."

"Great. Let's go."

Amaré placed the drone on the street, and we held our collective breaths, waiting for lift-off. With a quiet whir, it was airborne and sailing over the houses in front of us. Cassy held the phone with the relayed images, and we walked slowly behind it to keep it in our line of sight.

The backyards were unassuming—and dark. No one was outside sitting and talking, and even if they were, with the noise the cicadas were giving off we'd be lucky we could catch anything. Once we reached the fence of mystery neighbor two, Amaré spoke from behind us.

"Uh-oh."

"Whatchu mean, uh-oh?" Cassy asked.

"Shhh," I said. "What's wrong, Amaré?"

"Drone's gone," he said.

"What?" Cassy really didn't know how to whisper.

"Oh nooo," Sammie whispered next to me.

"Where'd you last see it?" I asked.

Amaré stared at me. "You're kidding, right? These yards all look the same."

"Damnit," I said. "You and Cassy go back the way we came, searching all the ground we covered, while Sammie and I go forward and see if it's in front of us.

We'll meet you at the car as soon as we can."

We split up, and Sammie and I pressed forward along the fence line ahead of us. I knew there would eventually be a gap at Haylee's house, so we would have to sprint across the space and hope for the best.

Just as we reached Haylee's house, the door opened, and she stepped outside—because, of course, she did. I could only pray the drone wasn't in her backyard. She was on her phone.

"I'm supposed to meet who?" *Pause.* "But why? They can't possibly think I had anything to do with this, can they?" *Pause.* "I know she works with your husband, but I don't like her. I don't like the way she looks at me. Like I'm her number one suspect. Fine. Yeah. Fine."

It didn't take a genius to know she was talking about me and that she was talking to Kristen Waters. She wasn't the first person to dislike me for the way I did my job, and she wouldn't be the last. In the dark, I felt Sammie's hand reach out and squeeze mine—I'm guessing she figured it out, too.

I thought Haylee would go back inside, but she sat there for about five minutes, which left Sammie and me no choice but to sit there and wait her out.

Finally, she got up and went inside, and the minute the door shut behind her, we booked it across the yard. We were three feet from the upcoming fence when the light in Haylee's backyard flicked on and the door opened and out came a massive black blur. Yep, it was a Rottweiler.

With no fence to contain him, he caught sight of us and took off at full speed, racing toward us. You could practically hear the wind whistling through his ears as he sprinted across the yard.

"Nice doggy," was all I got out before Sammie and I took off running. I wound up lost in the dark, running the wrong way and smacking into a sapling planted in the middle of the open space behind the houses. Sammie yanked my arm, and together we ran along the fence line, but before we reached the end, I tripped over a broken slat and fell flat on my face with Sammie a heartbeat behind me, falling directly on top of me.

"Are you okay?" I whispered.

"Yeah," Sammie drawled—not whispering. "Are we ready to leave yet? I'm done."

"Where'd the dog go?" I asked.

"She whistled for him, and he went back," Sammie said.

We turned toward the car with the light from our phones, but in the last few feet, Sammie slammed to a stop in front of me. Because I was watching where I was walking, I didn't see her stop in time and smacked into the back of her, which sent her forward—right into the path of a skunk. She didn't stand a chance. The skunk turned in the blink of an eye, took aim, and fired.

"Oh, sweet Moses, not this, too. Oh, no, no, no, no." All that praying was in vain because the skunk was now empty, and Sammie was full. We could hardly breathe because of the toxic cloud that emanated from such a small, cute animal. "Oh, merciful heavens. Holy cow!"

Trying unsuccessfully to contain my laughter but snorting anyway, I peered at Sammie with my dimmed phone light. If looks could kill, I would be so dead right now. "I'm so sorry. I just c-can't." Another fit of coughing and laughter overtook me, and I doubled over, trying to catch my breath.

"I'm going to come give you a hug in about two seconds if you don't quit that. How in tarnation am I going to get home now?"

My eyes were watering from the odor as well as the laughter and there were tears streaming down my face.

"Maybe Cassy or Amaré will have an idea," I said.

"Have an idea abou—what the hell is that?" Cassy finished the last more nasally than the first. My guess is because she was holding her nose against all that was Sammie right then.

"You all right, Ms. Sammie?" Amaré asked. He was such a gentleman.

"Thank you, Amaré, but I've been better. I don't know what to do. I don't want to smell up your c—so help me, Laci."

I couldn't help it. Really, I couldn't.

"Now, don't you worry about anything, Ms. Sammie. My car has seen much worse before, and I'm su—knock it off, Cass—I'm sure it will again."

"But—"

"If Amaré say it's okay, Sammie, then it's okay," Cassy said. "But if it's okay whichu, can you ride in the back? With the windows down?"

"Did you guys get the drone?" Sammie asked while we made our way back to the car.

"Yeah, we found it," Amaré said, "but we have to come back and get it another day."

"Wait, why?" I asked.

"It's up one of the pine trees that sit in the lot between the streets," he said. "We tried to shake it out, and someone tried to climb up and get it, but turns out she ain't so good at trees."

"Shut up," Cassy said.

And they were off and running. Amaré picked and Cassy dodged and vice versa, and they went round and round. Where the hell was the car?

"Amaré, are you ever going to get around to asking Cassy out?" I suddenly felt like playing the devil's advocate.

We walked a bit more in silence. Seriously, where were we parked?

"I'mma kill you when we get home, Laci, so help me Jesus," Cassy said.

"What?" I said. "I figured I would put out there what I've been wondering for a long time. You don't have to answer me, Amaré. I'm just being nosey."

I winked at Sammie under the light from a single lamppost in the middle of the black street. Cassy wasn't the only one who could rag their best friend on their relationships.

The silence the rest of the way to the car allowed my mind to wander. I wondered what Antonio was doing just then. It took everything in me not to bring out my phone and text him. I didn't think we were to casual texting just yet—even if I wanted us to be.

"Uh-oh," Amaré said.

"What's wrong?" I asked.

I looked to where he was pointing, and up ahead, mystery neighbor number three was on the move. They were dressed in Army OCPs and sticking to the shadows, but you could tell by the way they moved they had a goal in mind.

"Oh shit," Cassy said.

"I'm on it." I veered away from the group and

made my way to the pine tree in the middle of the grassy area. It was there that I met the woman in the OCPs. "Colonel Martin? I didn't know you lived on b—post."

Colonel Martin came to an abrupt halt and reared back like she'd been attacked. She round-house kicked the air in front of my face—missing me by inches. I think it was because she pulled the kick more than luck—but I wasn't going to argue with the result.

"Major Duvall?" she asked. "What on earth are you doing here?"

"Recon, ma'am," I said.

"Are you the one this drone belongs to?" she asked.

"Yes, ma'am. My team and I were investigating when the drone got away. We didn't have any luck retrieving it in the dark and were going to come back tomorrow."

"Hang tight, Major. I'll get it for you." She climbed the tree like she was a seven-year-old getting their kite out.

"Very impressive, ma'am," I said.

"Yes, well, getting up is one thing I can do well. It's getting down that's the tricky part," she said. "Here, catch."

I looked up in time to avoid a black eye but not in enough time to avoid batting it to the ground and hearing it crash the rest of the way to the grass. "Shit."

"Major, even I could have done that," she said. "Look out; I'm coming down."

And down she came. There were twigs snapping and needles flying and arms waving. I may have avoided the drone, but even I couldn't avoid a full bird colonel falling out of a tree directly on top of me.

"Fu—" *clunk*

"Are you okay, Major?

"If you could just get off my stomach, I think I could breathe a little better, Colonel," I wheezed.

"Laci?" Cassy ran up to us with Amaré a step behind, followed by Sammie bringing up the rear.

"Lord, what is that smell?" Colonel Martin asked. She rolled off me while swiveling her head where my friends stood beside us.

"That, Colonel, is the smell of adventure," I said.

"Well, it stinks," she said. She held her nose.

"Is it okay, Amaré? We didn't land on it, did we?" I asked.

"Nah, it's okay. Thank you for getting it, ma'am," he said.

"Oh, is that yours?" She eyed him. "Who are you anyway?"

"Officer Amaré Green, Baltimore City Police Department."

"Can I get your phone number?" she asked. "You know. For the paperwork?"

I bit back a grin and glanced at Cassy while Amaré relayed the information to Colonel Martin. Served her right. She needed a swift kick in the ass to get her to do something about him.

Once we said goodnight to Colonel Martin, we were able to load back into the car and set out for home. We hadn't discovered much tonight, except that Haylee wasn't looking forward to meeting me, but then when you're a prime suspect when do you look forward to seeing the one who could put you away?

Chapter Fifteen

With a sense of déja vu, I interrupted Beethoven the following morning before he really got a chance to get to the good part. What could I say—I like a variety of music.

"What?" I asked.

"Klingons and clam shells, Major," Colonel Waters said. Five o'clock a.m.—should I be thankful for the extra hour this morning?

"What's happened, sir?" I asked.

"Someone got to the old lady. Jill's neighbor… what's her name?"

"Mrs. Zimmer, sir?"

"Yeah, her. She's on her way to Franklin Square. I told them you'd be there ASAP. Colonel Martin is expecting you. This is now top priority."

"Yes, sir. On my way."

I didn't bother changing and just slapped a sweatshirt on top of my gym shorts and shoved my feet into slippers. I grabbed Sammie's keys from the front door and tripped outside. Again.

Thankfully, I lived around the corner from the hospital, so I was through the front door in no time. If I had taken longer, I might have missed Wesley trying to sweet talk her way to the back. Instead, I stepped in front of her at the Information Desk and gave my name. The receptionist called to the back and told me they

159

would be right there.

"You're free to go, Hanscom," I said.

Instead of leaving, she eased into parade rest and folded her arms across her chest and tried to stare me down. Silly girl. Didn't she know that bigger men than her had tried and failed to intimidate me?

Dr. Tangen spoke my name from the door, and I turned from Hanscom to follow him. I knew, without even looking, that she was behind me. When I reached the door, I told her again to leave.

"No," she said.

"What did you say?" I rounded on her like a wrestler in the ring. It seemed we were indeed going to do this here and now. That's okay. I was ready. "You know, *Captain*, I have been nice to a fault with you. I have gone out of my way to be courteous and civil. I have gone by the book. I have followed the chain of command. I have done everything the Air Force has told me to do, but you know what, *Captain*? You don't listen. Apparently, there is a rule book just for you that the Air Force doesn't know about.

"Well, as of this moment, Captain, I will be playing by *my* rules. And rule number one says that I can write an LOR for you as soon as I am back in the office. Oh, yes, I see by the look on your face you know what that is. And as your supervisor it is entirely within my job description to correct and instruct my subordinate who is not upholding the standard of performance, conduct, or integrity, and I must say you haven't been displaying any of these characteristics, have you?

"Now, before I can think of something else I may want to add, I suggest you gather your little things, walk to your car, and go home. Have I made myself clear, *Captain*?"

The shock on her face was mildly satisfying, and I would have enjoyed it if I wasn't so angry. The door opening behind me and nudging me in the back broke the spell between us, and Wesley turned and practically sprinted from the building.

"Major?" Dr. Tangen asked.

"Right here, sir. Sorry about that—just doing my own housekeeping. What can you tell me has happened?"

"Older woman, in her sixties, came in with a case of fentanyl overdose. Her husb—"

"How do you know it's fentanyl?" I asked.

"Her nephew is an EMT and cam—Oh my goodness."

We sprinted the rest of the way to the room. When we burst inside, it was empty except for Mrs. Zimmer and her husband sitting next to her, holding her hand. He was crying.

"Where's your nephew?" I asked.

"He's not here. Why?"

"He was here," Dr. Tangen said. "He came in with her on the ambulance. Where did he go?"

Dr. Tangen shot out the door and I stayed with Mr. Zimmer to question him.

"Do you know if he left with the ambulance to return to work?" I asked.

"I don't know. He must have. He doesn't have a car here. What's going on?"

"Give me a moment." I left the room to find Dr. Tangen and see if he had any luck finding the escape artist nephew. Two steps outside the door and around the corner to the right, I collided with Colonel Martin. "Oh, good, it's you," I said. "Go in that room and stay with Mr. and Mrs. Zimmer. I'll be right back."

I shoved her to the door and left for the nurse's station, where they told me which direction Dr. Tangen went. I then ran through the curtained-off areas to where the ER emptied outside. He was coming back when I reached him.

"Already gone, huh?" I asked.

"Missed him by two minutes," he said. "I called over the radio, but they wouldn't answer."

"Can we call 911 on a rogue ambulance?" I asked.

"Too dramatic," he said. "He could be on another call already."

"I left the Zimmers with Colonel Martin. Mr. Zimmer is in the dark on why we're asking about his nephew. At this point, it's all conjecture on our part, but I think it's best if we stay as vague as possible when we're talking about his nephew. We don't need him tipping him off any more than we already have."

We stopped outside the Zimmers' door, and Dr. Tangen turned to leave.

"I've got other places to be this morning, so I'll leave them with you. I'll check with Mrs. Zimmer later."

Before I pushed my way inside the room, a movement behind the retreating Dr. Tangen caught my eye, and who should be standing ten yards away, but one Antonio Desio. He didn't see me, and before I decided if I wanted him to or not, he glanced up and caught me looking at him. He seemed as surprised to see me as I was him. But just showing you how my luck is, the door opened behind me, and Colonel Martin grabbed my arm and yanked me inside. The last I saw was the astonished look on Antonio's face.

"Why did you leave me alone with him?" I don't think Colonel Martin knew how to whisper any more than Cassy did. If she did, she forgot.

"Isn't this your job?" I asked.

"Yes, but usually it's not people who are comatose or one who wishes he was. This guy hasn't stopped bemoaning his fate since I walked in."

"Did you try talking to him?"

"You know—I do know how to do my job," she said.

Just then, the door hit me in the back, and I cursed my luck even more.

"Laci?" Antonio asked.

"Laci?" Colonel Martin asked.

"Ant—Desio," I said.

"Aunt Desio?" Colonel Martin asked.

I stepped aside and the door opened, and Antonio walked in in all his glory. He was a lot to take in, and boy, did Colonel Martin take him in. He was looking especially fine today in a pair of fancy Italian shoes, jeans, an untucked button-down, and a cardigan. Cardigan, really? "Where the hell is your gun? Uh—Detective Antonio Desio, let me introduce you to Colonel Carol Martin, Commander for the Army CID. Colonel Martin, this is Baltimore City Police Detective Antonio Desio. Desio, we're here for work. Did you need something?"

He blinked around the room for a second, looked at me again, then turned for the door. "Not a thing, not a damn thing."

I snorted, and he left.

"Antonio?" Colonel Martin asked.

"It's a long story." I glanced behind her at Mr. Zimmer. I didn't feel like having this conversation now—if ever. "Mr. Zimmer, I'm Major Laci Duval with Air Force Office of Special Investigation, and this is—"

"I know who she is," Mr. Zimmer said. "My wife has told me all about her."

I turned to Colonel Martin to see how she took that, and if the look of surprise was anything to go on, then it was news to her as well. We turned as a unit to the punctured tea bag sitting in the chair by his wife. You could practically feel the leaves under your feet when we approached him in his chair.

"Yes, well, what can you tell us happened to Mrs. Zimmer?"

"I wish to God I knew," he said. "She was beside herself this morning with worry about something but wouldn't tell me. She and that girl with the big dog were out talking in front of the house late last night."

"Big dog? The Rottweiler?" At his look of confusion, I went on. "No tail? Black?"

"Yes, yes, that's the one. Then this morning, I can't wake her up, so I called 911."

"Did you hear her up before you? Any time in the middle of the night?" Colonel Martin asked.

"No," Mr. Zimmer sniffed. I'd heard that kind of sniff of disdain before. Recently too. It was the kind Floyd Wheaton gave me when he had to give an answer, but he didn't want to talk to me. I wondered what was eating him. I turned to Colonel Martin and slid my eyes to the door—hoping she would catch my drift. Maybe I could kill two birds with one stone.

"I'm going to find the doc, if you'll excuse me," she said.

"Mr. Zimmer," I said once Colonel Martin was gone. "I wonder if you could enlighten me about what it is your wife has told you about Colonel Martin?"

His eyes grew large instantly. He didn't like being put on the spot and called on his shit. I didn't have time for childishness. I needed Colonel Martin's help, and if he couldn't work with her, then we had a problem.

"My sweet Betsey told me all about the shenanigans that go on at Colonel Martin's house. Men are like tissues to her—they're a dime a dozen."

"Why do you care?" I asked.

"Because my wife cares?" He sounded genuinely baffled that I didn't make the connection.

"What can you tell me about the relationship your wife has with Haylee Bishop?"

"Haylee? What's she got to do with this?" he asked.

"If you please, sir, just answer the question."

"Haylee has been a godsend. She's there when Betsey needs someone to talk to or needs someone to run to the PX for her. She does odd jobs around the house, too. When I was down with my back last month, she mowed the lawn for us. Such a sweet girl."

"Does Haylee talk about the spouse's club or Jill or Ruby to you any?"

"She just shared the news of the election."

"Did you know about the animosity between Jill and Ruby?"

"Who's Ruby? She the dead one?" he asked.

"No, Jill is the dead one. Ruby is the neighbor on the other side of Jill."

"Oh. No, I don't know her."

"Can you tell me the address for your nephew the EMT?" I asked.

"He's not my nephew—he's Betsey's. I don't care for him, to be honest. High school drop-out. Got his GED because she harassed him. He lives somewhere in the city."

"Baltimore? What's his name? Do you know?"

"Yeah. Ted Stone. That's all I'm saying about him." He sniffed again. Maybe he really was sick. I hoped his pomposity wasn't contagious.

"That's all I want to know. I'm going to go find Colonel Martin. I'll be sure and check back in before I leave."

I practically tripped over her when I pulled the door open.

"Where's your glass?" I grinned at her before she punched me. "Ow."

"What'd he say?"

"Mrs. Zimmer thought you should put a revolving door up on the front of your house for all the men you go through and shared that view with her husband."

I never thought Colonel Martin could be embarrassed, but she turned pink right in front of me, and her eyes teared up. "I—I—"

"Hey, it doesn't matter to me what a nosey old bat says. Dating is hard as hell in this day and age."

"Says the one who has someone already. Or am I mistaken with my brief assessment of you and the Charm City heartthrob back there?"

Now it was my turn to turn pink. "Yeah, well, it's complicated. Remind me to tell you about it over a strong drink someday."

"It's a deal." She stuck her hand out for me to shake. "And I'll tell you about the one I made go away."

"Deal—" We were mid-shake when Dr. Tangen came around the corner with a clipboard in his hand and a frown on his face. "What's up, doc?" I asked. Colonel Martin kicked me.

"We're going to put Mrs. Zimmer into a medically induced coma. Between the overdose and her age, we need to do something fast to get the swelling in her brain down. There's a chance it could be irreversible, but without inducing the coma, prospects are slim for a recovery. I'm on my way to tell her husband now."

"Oh, shit," I said.

Dr. Tangen let out a loud sigh, and his shoulders drooped. "Yeah. I don't like doing these things."

"Sorry, doctor," Colonel Martin said.

"I'll step inside with you while you tell him," I said, "but then I'm going to need to leave. I have one car, and my roommate needs it to get her kids to school."

"I can stay," Colonel Martin said.

"You sure?" I asked.

"Yep, you did it last time."

"Okay, just let Mr. Zimmer know I had to go then. Thanks. We'll catch up and compare notes later on."

Before I left the building I called and left a message for Desio to do a look-up on Ted Stone to see if he could find out anything on him for me. I needed a last known address, phone number, anything that could help me locate him.

I also needed to formulate a plan on Haylee Bishop. She was the last known person to speak with

Betsey Zimmer, and she was at Ruby's house before each of them suffered an overdose. She was showing up way too often for my taste. It was past time to call her into the sheriff's office.

Chapter Sixteen

I may have ruined a prospective friendship with Kristen Waters the next day when I called to tell her I didn't need help talking to Haylee.

"Why don't you need my help anymore, Major?" Kristen asked.

"Because she's being summoned to the sheriff's office this morning for official questioning in the death and possible poisoning of others. I'm not really supposed to be talking to you about it. I just wanted you to hear it from me, though."

I tried to soften the blow, but we still both hung up, unhappy with the situation. Now, here I was hours later, speaking to Haylee.

Sammie dropped the twins off at school and rushed back so I could have the car in time to get to my morning meeting. I would then need to rush back to the house so she could get the kids at the end of the day. I didn't expect this to take as long as all that, but you never knew.

Deputy Robinson, Colonel Martin, Captain Dan, and Haylee Bishop, and the representative from the Army Trial Defense Services, Major Malachi Barnes, and I were gathered around the conference table at the Harford County Sheriff's office in Edgewood. It was neutral ground and served to show Haylee that she wasn't under arrest but was indeed a suspect in multiple cases. Everyone looked to me to begin.

"Haylee, when I met you alongside Miles and Candice, you said you didn't know Jill until you got here. Miles said you told him that you were stationed with her previously. Can you clarify for me which is correct?"

"Umm, I think I was nervous that day meeting with you. I didn't know what I was saying. We were stationed with Jill and Noah at Bragg in North Carolina."

"Were you stationed there the same time Ruby and Damian were also there?" I asked.

"Ummm, I think so," she said.

Hmmm.

"Major, if I may," Deputy Robinson said. "I'm going to jump ahead to the day of Mrs. Westfall's death. Can you tell us where you were when the deceased was found in the bathroom?"

"I was with Ruby at my car," she said.

"Actually," I said, "according to Ruby, you left her because of a phone call. Ruby ended up taking the box of papers back to the tent by herself because she couldn't find you anywhere. In addition to Deputy Robinson's question, I want to know why those papers were needed that day. According to Miles, they weren't even necessary for that event."

Haylee looked flustered and confused, and her husband looked mad. "Could you give us a minute?" Major Barnes asked.

"Sure." I stayed seated. If they needed a minute, then they could be the ones who left the room. Sure enough, after a glance at us not moving, they got up.

"This is not looking so good for Mrs. Bishop,"

Colonel Martin said.

"I've seen worse get off scot-free," Deputy Robinson said.

A few minutes later, the door opened, and everyone took their places. Haylee no longer looked ready to cry, but she didn't look like someone ready to admit she'd murdered either.

"My client is willing to submit a polygraph test to prove her innocence," Major Barnes said.

"I didn't know we'd gotten that far already," Colonel Martin said.

"Let's be real, Colonel," Major Barnes said. "You have no other suspects, and your hopes are pinned on Mrs. Bishop here. I say we nip this in the bud and save us all a lot of time and headache."

"I still want my questions answered before we get to the polygraph," I said. "And since we're all here, I want them answered now."

"Fine," Major Barnes said. "But I reserve the right to halt the interview at any point."

"Fine. Haylee, why did you go see Ruby the night before she went to the hospital? And what time was it?"

"I went as a friend seeing a friend. There was no underlying reason. Mrs. Zimmer was there when I got there. Wouldn't leave off trying to get her to take her anxiety meds. Once the old bat left, I thought I talked her out of it, but sometime in the night, she must have decided she needed them after all. I wish she'd have called me instead. I told her she could."

"If you feel that way about Mrs. Zimmer, then why did you go see her the other night?" I asked.

"I like to keep my friends close but my enemies closer," Haylee said. "It's the way I was with Jill and

171

the way I am with Mrs. Zimmer."

"What do you know about Mrs. Zimmer's nephew?" I asked.

"Ted?" When I nodded, she went on. "He's a bit of a deadbeat, but he's okay. She adores him and paid for him to go on a vacation—I don't know where. That was before all this happened, though. Why?"

"Just curious. Back to my previous question. Why were the membership papers included in the box the day Jill was found?"

"You'd have to ask Jill that one," Haylee said. "It was what she told me to do."

"Why did you designate yourself the go-between for Jill and Ruby? What was in it for you?"

"That's enough, Major," Captain Bishop erupted from his chair.

"I think it's a fair question," I said. "Considering someone is dead."

"There was nothing in it for me," Haylee said. "I did it because I liked Ruby, and she was my friend. I wouldn't hurt her. Not ever."

"That's all I have for now, but I may have more later," I said. "I'll also have a list of questions for the polygraph by the end of the day, Sheriff."

I left the room and racked my brain for the answer to the puzzle I was left with now. If Haylee didn't hurt Ruby, would she have hurt Jill to protect Ruby? Did someone else hurt Jill? Did someone else hurt Jill and Ruby, and are making it look like Haylee did it?

"What did you think of all she had to say?" Colonel Martin asked.

I leaned against the side of Sammie's car and thought about that.

"You know, I don't know. I think some of what she said is the truth, and I think some is what she thinks is the truth, but I also think some is a stretch even by our standards. You know?"

"Yeah, but the hard part is figuring out which is which," Colonel Martin said. "What questions do you suggest for the polygraph?"

"You want to put our heads together and see what we can come up with? We can hop up the road a bit and stop in at the brother's pizza shop. I think they're open this early," I said.

"Sounds good. I'll follow you."

We went up the road less than a mile and found the local sub and pizza shop was open and grabbed a couple slices of NY pizza. It was really good. The kind where you lick the oil off your fingers and stretch the cheese.

Once we settled in with our slices and soda, I never mixed pizza with sweet tea, I dug out my notepad and pen and got to work. Colonel Martin gave my rustic measures the side-eye, but I wasn't explaining my methods just then.

"I think we need to start by double-checking if she actually was on the phone at the time she walked away from Ruby at the car the morning Jill was found in the bathroom," I spoke while I took notes.

"Tell her the records can be obtained showing whether she was on the phone at that time," Colonel Martin said. "Sometimes that alone will have them willingly submitting their records."

"Good idea," I said. "Did she see Jill the morning she died? I don't know if she's been asked that yet."

"If she didn't kill her, did she know anyone who

might have a reason to?" Colonel Martin said.

"She also never answered where she was while she was on the phone those few minutes before Jill was found," I said. "If we knew who she was talking to, it could help her—or hurt her."

Thirty-five questions later, Colonel Martin and I wrapped things up. We said goodbye, and I jogged out the door to the car. I'd drop these off at the sheriff's office on my way through. Lucky for me, when I entered the building off Route 40, Deputy Robinson was walking in the lobby.

"What'd you think of the interview?" he asked.

"I think there's a lot that's missing," I said. I recounted my conversation with Colonel Martin and what we discussed before handing over the paper with the list of questions.

"You don't want to be here for the questioning?" he asked.

"Not if I don't have to be," I said. "I trust you. Let me know the results once you've finished, though."

"Will do."

****

It was nice to have the house to myself, even if it was just for an hour or so. I got home in time for Sammie to stop by her parents' house before she went and got the kids. Cassy tagged along to get out after being cooped up all morning. I'd told her she could always get Amaré to stop by and get her if she was desperate to get out, but then she'd shown me what she thought of that idea.

I took Needles into the backyard as a treat for me and him, and Boo followed us so she could stretch her legs and lie in the sunshine. The weather was August hot, and there wasn't a cloud in the sky, but there was humidity in abundance.

When Beethoven's Ninth blasted through the house and out the back door, I was brought back to reality. I reached it before it began again for the third time or hung up. I wasn't sure.

"Major Duvall," I said.

"Well, you've stepped in it this time," Colonel Waters said. "No. No. Don't talk. She's gone and done it. She's opened a CDI on you. Mule muffins, Major, what in Hattie's hell did you do?"

I was too stunned to speak for once, but only for a second.

"I didn't do anything, sir. I threatened her with an LOR, but I haven't gotten around to writing it yet. But you can bet your sweet bippy I'm going to now, though."

"No, you will not, Major. It will look like retaliation, and that is one thing we don't need right now. Let her look like the crazy one she is. Do you understand me? You are to sit on this and stay away from her. Do you hear me?"

"Yes, sir. I hear you, sir. Then keep her away from me. I have not *once* gone looking for her, sir, but everywhere I go, there she is."

"I don't care if you look for her like a kid looks for presents before Christmas or if she just appears like a magician's rabbit. If she shows her face—you leave. If she walks in—you walk out. Do *not* give her the opportunity to say or do anything to you. I can't believe I am having this conversation. You would think I was a kindergarten teacher instead of a commander of grown-ass adults. Stay away, Major. That's an order."

"Yes, sir," I spoke to empty air because he was gone. I couldn't believe the nerve of that woman—a CDI? Really? A CDI is a Command Directive Investigation, and it means no stone would be left unturned when trying to validate or invalidate her claims against me. I knew in my heart that nothing would come of it, but it made me nervous anyway.

The doorbell rang before I cleared the hanging screen at the back door, so I did an about-face and returned to the front of the house. I wasn't sure if I was glad to see Antonio or upset when I pulled open the door and found him on my small porch.

"Hello, Antonio. To what do I owe the honor?" I asked.

"You called and left me a message, so I thought I'd drop by since I was in the area," he said.

"What are you doing up this way?" I asked.

"Coming to see you."

"I'm surprised you're alone today." I didn't know why I felt like poking the bear, but it just came to me. Maybe it was the angst I felt coming from Colonel Waters, but I was suddenly in a pouty mood.

"Is that really how you want this conversation to go?" he asked.

My shoulders slumped. He was right—he didn't deserve that. I silently waved him into my office, where we sat down, and I unloaded everything on him. It felt good to talk to him about the case. I didn't realize I needed to share it with him until then. I'd missed this. My last case, we'd worked together, and I think I missed sharing things with him.

"So, where do you stand with everything now?"

"Now that is the million-dollar question," I said.

"Then you're really not going to like the news I have for you," he said. "The address I have for Ted Stone is an empty lot next to our favorite club."

"The Purple Pelican?" I asked.

"Yep."

"That's really weird. Did you ask Zucca if he's heard of him?"

"No, I figured you'd want to join me on that outing. How about it? You up for a trip?"

"Since you've got the wheels, sure."

I closed the back door and put Needles in the kitchen before grabbing my bag from the front table. I slammed to a stop outside my front door because instead of the normal police sedan, Antonio was driving a monster truck.

"What the hell is that?" I asked.

"Donated."

"You have got to be kidding me." I slowly approached the truck, and the top of the tire came to my chin. No kidding.

"You can't make this stuff up," he said.

"How the hell am I supposed to get in?" Antonio stood next to me and looped his hands down around my calf, and I stared at the top of his head. "You did this on purpose, didn't you? So you could stare at my ass when I'm struggling to get in?"

He started laughing before he stood up and kept going when he was upright next to me. He threw his head back, and there were honest-to-God tears coming out. I would have laughed too, but I was too surprised by what I was seeing.

"I never even considered that, Laci." He wiped his eyes with his hands. "I swear—it's just a bonus. Now, come on."

He repeated the action, and I placed my foot in his hands. Then, he threw me up in the air, and I landed inside the truck cab with plenty of room to spare. In fact, I almost made it into the driver's seat there was so much heave behind his ho.

Antonio had no problem hauling himself into the truck, and we were soon on our way downtown. Before we got too far, I sent Cassy a text letting her know I was out on assignment.

It was amazing what you could see when you sat so far above everyone else on the road. As we approached the tunnel, I swore we would hit the roof—which did wonders for my nerves.

Trust me, being closer to God did not calm down my anxiety, and my eyes were constantly scanning every nook and cranny of the tunnel for a leak. If this thing broke down Antonio was on his own.

There were two things in life I was afraid of. Cold-calling people was one, and the second was tunnels. Antonio reached over and took my hand and held it the last half of the tunnel—he knew how I felt in there. I thought he would release it once we were out the other side, but he surprised me by holding onto it until we reached the club.

We pulled into the half-empty parking lot of the Purple Pelican in the early afternoon. We were sure to miss the night show, but there would be dancers and regulars mingling about the place this time of day. I hoped Zucca was there, but if he wasn't, I knew where his other office was located.

After I took a leap from the truck and landed safely on the blacktop, we made our way inside the darkened club. There was a handful of people at the bar to the right, and I nodded to Adam, the bartender. We skirted the tables and booths in the middle of the room and approached Zucca's office in the back left corner. The music was hushed, and the stage was empty. Must be an off day.

I knocked once and let myself in. Luca was mid-stride on his way to the door, but I looked past him to where Zucca sat behind his desk.

"You know yous could wait until you're let in," Luca said.

"It's all right, Luca," Zucca said. "How can I help you, Major?"

"We're looking for Ted Stone," I said. "He listed his address as the lot next door to the club. I realize that doesn't mean anything, but I thought I'd ask just in case."

"Do you have a picture?" Zucca asked.

"I don't," I said. "Do you have one, Desio?" He shook his head. "He's an EMT in Harford County. That's all I know about him. That and he can get his hands on fentanyl pretty easily, it seems. He has an aunt and uncle who live on Aberdeen who take care of him, but I don't know anything about his parents."

"That doesn't ring a bell for me. Does it for you, Luca?"

"Nope."

"Is it okay if I ask Adam on my way out?"

"That's okay with me," Zucca said. "Thank you for asking. Have a nice day."

With that, he returned his attention to his papers in front of him. I guessed we were finished. We left the room, and I crossed to the bar where Adam was wiping something off a spotless bar top.

"Hiya, Adam, long time no see," I said.

"Yeah."

"Can you tell me if you know anyone by the name of Ted Stone?" I asked.

For the briefest of seconds, Adam's face froze, but in the next it was gone. When he spoke, it was with a strangely neutral tone, too.

"Nope, can't say I know that name. Why?"

"He's connected to a case I'm working in Aberdeen. His address is listed as the adjacent lot next door, so we're looking into it. I'll be in touch. Thanks."

I caught Antonio's eye when I turned from the bar, and we left the club. He raised his eyebrows, which could mean he caught on too. There was something wrong with Adam's answers. Good to know.

"Did you catch that?" I asked.

"The bartender's face tightening? Yeah—subtle but noticeable."

"If only we knew what it meant," I said. "Which side of the club is Ted's address?"

From in front of the truck and facing the club, Saratoga Street ran behind us. Antonio's parent's restaurant was around the corner in Little Italy. It had been years since I'd been there.

"It's the Jones Falls Expressway lot next to the club," Antonio said.

"Well, damn. It's just an empty parking lot. I hoped there would be something helpful here."

"There might be. Look."

Antonio stared at the side of the club. We shuffled behind the truck tire and saw Adam on his phone. With the Expressway behind us, it was hard to make out what he was saying, but it didn't take a genius to see he was adamant about something. Adam opened the door of a small hatchback and climbed into the driver's seat.

"I wish I knew what he was saying," I said.

"Your super hearing doesn't work that way, huh?"

"Nope. I can recognize voices and hear better than most, but even I can't hear over traffic noise immediately behind me. Can you guys call him in for questioning?"

"For what?"

"I'm sure you can come up with something." I gave him a Cheshire cat grin. "Let's go ask Zucca."

"Ask him what?" But I was already across the parking lot and at the front door. I didn't have an answer either. I figured maybe Zucca could find something out if we couldn't.

I knocked and let myself in again. This time, Luca just gave me a dirty look, but he didn't hold it like he did before.

"Back so soon, Major?" Zucca asked.

"We never left. What can you tell me about Adam Wilhite? The bartender?"

"Why?"

"I'm pretty sure he lied to me when I questioned him about Ted. I want to know why he lied, and I also want to know who he was arguing with in the parking lot once we left. My hunch is it was Ted."

"Luca," Zucca said. It was all he needed to say, and the big boy got up and left. "If you two would be so kind and wait in the back room over there?"

Zucca nodded his chin at a door diagonal to his desk on the left. He didn't need to ask us twice. We slipped inside and closed the door behind us. It was a small dark closet. Oh yeah, that's the third thing I was afraid of—small, dark spaces. About the time I started breathing through my mouth to keep from passing out, I felt Antonio's hand in mine, and his lips went to my forehead. He remembered my reaction to these places. He didn't drive out the demons, but it toned down my response to them.

Before I knew it, I broke through my feelings and on to something else. Antonio's lips were on my neck and up again, where they met mine head on. *Woah.* I did not see that coming. He put his arms around my waist and pulled me to him with a tug. I went gladly— not really believing this was happening. We were supposed to be listening to the conversation on the other side of the door. They could open it any—*oh my*.

Wait. Where were my hands? Oh, Lordy, they were anchored in his hair. When did I put them in there? The sudden groan had us springing apart. Was that him or me? Turns out it was neither, but it brought us back to our senses. And just in time, it seemed.

Luca yanked open the door. "You twos can come out now."

"What happened to him?" I asked. This was good. If I focused on something else, my face wouldn't betray me.

Adam was out cold, spread eagle on the floor of the office. In addition to the pulse I felt in his wrist, he sported a bruise that was quickly surfacing on his jaw.

"He ran into my fist," Luca said.

"Really?" I asked. "Why did you have a fist in the vicinity of his face?"

"He upset me greatly."

"What did he say? Did he know Ted Stone?"

Antonio asked.

"Mr. Stone is a dealer," Zucca said. "He denied purchasing anything from Mr. Stone but refused my request for a drug test. When I informed him his employment depended on it, he became agitated, and it was then that he met his fate at the end of Luca's arm."

"Wow. Did he say what Ted deals?" I asked.

"Not really. Does it matter?" Zucca asked.

"It might," I said. "I have two women in the hospital with fentanyl overdoses, both linked to Ted. One is in a coma, and one may lose her baby because of it."

"That was all I could get out of him, and until I can get a drug test from him, I really have nothing to show to the police."

"Thanks anyway," I said. "Can you keep us informed of Adam's whereabouts and if you see or hear about Ted from the dancers?"

"I will, yes," Zucca said.

I felt like a busted balloon as we left the office and club. All the fun and games were over, and I still had no way to link Ted Stone to Haylee. Antonio helped me into the truck, and we drove back to my house in silence.

Chapter Seventeen

Antonio dropped me off on Philadelphia Road. I didn't feel like the hassle I knew would come if the girls saw him with me. Plus, I felt our moment in the closet was written all over my face, and I couldn't explain the momentary lapse in judgment.

I was mentally and physically exhausted, and it wasn't even dinner time. I dragged myself the distance to the house, which I swear doubled under the weight of my exhaustion. The chaos inside the front door wrapped me in a warm hug, and I picked up Ana on my way to the couch.

She babbled on about school with only a word here and there recognizable. I leaned my head against the back of the couch and closed my eyes. This wasn't like me. The girls knew it, and I knew it, but there wasn't a damn thing they could do to help me.

I replayed the conversations of the day and tried to fit the pieces together. I didn't know if I was missing something or not. I just knew I was no closer to figuring this all out now than I was last week.

Ted Stone was the wild card. I didn't know where he fit into this. He was connected to both Mrs. Zimmer and to Haylee, but I couldn't connect him to Jill except through those two women. For that matter he didn't connect to Ruby except through Haylee and Mrs. Zimmer either. How, you ask? Because of the medicine bottles. In both cases, he was the one who removed the medicine bottles. The question then becomes, did one of these two women—or someone else—want him to remove the bottles, or was he in it on his own? I could ask one, but as of yet, I couldn't ask the other. And, for that matter, how could I be so sure Ted was involved? Simple—my gut told me, and my time serving in the Air Force assured me just how reliable my gut was.

Somewhere in the midst of my wonderings and Ana's baby talk, I fell asleep. It wasn't a restful one, either. It was full of dark rooms and Italian men. I woke up on my side around one with my stomach yelling at me, so I got up to grab something to eat. The lights were off, and Needles was on his big blue pillow in the kitchen, with the light above the stove revealing his silhouette. He stood when he heard me get up from the couch.

"Hiya, boy," I whispered.

I stepped over the gate, opened the fridge to grab leftovers with one hand, and pushed the button to open the microwave with the other. There was a couple of days' worth of dinner in the fridge—we didn't believe in throwing things away around here. At last, I breathed in the smell of spaghetti carbonara as well as some pomodoro and had my mouth full when there was a light tapping on the front door. I knew who it would be, without a doubt.

"You must have smelled the Italian food," I spoke around a mouthful to Antonio when I opened the door.

He gave me his crooked smile and came in. "Is that what you're eating?"

"Yep. You want some?"

"Did you make it?"

"Of course," I said. "I'm teaching Sammie how to do it the true Italian Nonna way."

"You don't smack her hand when she does it wrong, do you?"

"Your Nonna would smack you for saying that, and you know it." I laughed.

"Who's here?" Cassy asked from the top of the stairs.

"Just Antonio, Cass. We're eating. Do you want any?"

"Hell, yeah." She hopped from two steps up and joined us at the table. We no sooner had the food on our plates than Sammie stuck her head around the corner of the landing.

"What are y'all doing? Don't you know what time it is?"

"We're eating the food you made. Do you want some before it's all gone?" I asked.

"Well, of course, silly."

She grabbed a plate and joined us at the table and our little family was complete, except for the kiddos. And Rev. Somehow, Antonio fit in without even trying. The table even looked empty when he wasn't the— wait. When did that happen?

"What happened today?" Cassy asked. "You wasn' in a place to ask when you got home, so I'm askin' now."

Antonio and I recounted everything we'd discovered during the day, leaving out the part in the closet.

"So, now we're stuck with no way to find Ted or to even find out what happened to Adam," I said.

"Well, shit," Cassy said. "I can do that. When I

start my job at the Purple Pelican, I'll keep an eye out for Adam and this Ted dude. The trick is talkin' to the dancers and seein' what they know. Maybe they be helpful, maybe they won'. I think if I can get in good with them, they might be more willing to talk, you know?"

"That's perfect, Cassy. Any information you can find on him would help."

"Just be careful," Antonio said. "We don't know what it is we're dealing with yet."

"I wish I knew if he was responsible for Jill's death or not, but for the life of me, other than Mrs. Zimmer and Haylee, I can't figure the link between them. Antonio, are you going to be okay going home? Do you want to stay here?" At the silence, I looked around the table and I realized what I'd said out loud. "On the couch, I mean."

"Uh-huh," Cassy said. "*On the couch.*" Cassy did a poor job of imitating me, but she didn't care. She just laughed and put her dishes in the dishwasher before heading back to bed with Sammie a step behind her.

"Sorry about that." I put my dishes on the counter by Antonio, then walked him down the hall to the front door. "How is it you tend to be here this late at night so often? Do you live in the row behind me?"

Instead of answering me he gave me his mysterious smile, kissed me on the forehead, then walked to his car—his regular car—and hopped in. He wasn't going to satisfy my curiosity just then. I'd let him remain an enigma a little bit longer, but sooner or later, he'd have to tell me.

****

The next morning, I slept in. It was nice not to

wake up to my phone yelling at me while I tripped over the cat and rushed to get out the door. Instead, I chose the leisurely route of a shower, breakfast out back with Needles, Ana, Ryan, and Boo, and then walking to my home office to get some paperwork done.

There was no way I would step foot inside the Field Investigation Squadron-Operating Location or FIS OL if I could help it. I had no intention of upsetting Colonel Waters further. I could do everything I needed from my home office. So, that's what I would do.

First on my to-do list was to contact Deputy Robinson to see how the polygraph went with Haylee yesterday. I wasn't one to put my eggs all in one basket where these were concerned, but sometimes they could surprise you and open up new avenues of questioning.

When I couldn't reach him in the office, I left a message and got back to work on separating emails into groups. Immediately, can wait, and garbage. The three from Asher could definitely wait since he was building up to something—I just didn't know what it was yet.

The one that caught my eye and was of utmost importance was the official notice from Colonel Waters for my CDI. It looked like Hanscom was wasting no time.

Wesley felt I'd *Abused Authority* in trying to get her off my case. That was all she had. Colonel Waters set the suspense date for ten duty days from today. I didn't think it would take that long, but I wouldn't put it past Hanscom to try and drag it out so she could get her way. All I needed to do was answer the questions of the Investigating Officer (IO) whenever they called and do my job in the meantime.

A sudden wave of weariness settled over me, and I

placed my forehead on my folded arms on my desk. Which is where Cassy found me a minute later.

"Wha's wrong whichu?" she asked.

"Captain Hanscom has opened an investigation into me. I don't think anything will come of it, but there's always the chance."

"Why? What happened?"

"She thinks by me telling her it's my case that I'm abusing my authority, but really I'm not. I'm just trying to do my job."

"It takes all kinds, I guess," Cassy said. "Well, I called Zucca, and I start my job today. I figured I'd wait till I got there before I tell him anythin' more—if then."

"He's smart. He may have figured it out already," I said.

"True dat."

I held my finger up to Cassy so I could grab my phone out of my purse, where it was blaring. "Major Duval."

"Good morning, Major, this is Deputy Robinson. I would love to give you the results of the polygraph, but I can't. Mrs. Bishop never showed up to take it."

"Wait—what? She didn't show up? Why didn't you call me?" I asked. "I could have contacted someone on APG."

"Because I kept thinking she would show up, but I figured by the end of the day when she wasn't there, then she wasn't coming at all. Let me know what you find out, and I'll schedule another."

"Damnit." I jammed my finger down on the disconnect on my phone then threw it on my desk.

"What happened?" Cassy asked.

"Haylee didn't show up for the polygraph test."

"Oh no, tha's not suspicious at all," Cassy said.

"I need to call Colonel Martin." I grabbed my phone, and Cassy about-faced into the kitchen and from the banging I heard while on hold, it sounded like she was preparing breakfast.

"Colonel Martin," she said.

"Good morning, Colonel. Do you know where I can find Haylee Bishop—she didn't show up for the polygraph yesterday."

"And you're just now telling me?" she said.

"Ma'am, I only found out a few minutes ago. Did you see any movement at her house when you left this morning?"

"Major, unlike others on my street, I don't pay attention to what my neighbors are doing. I'll look around and see what I can find. I'll check on her husband at his office."

"Thank you. I'll talk to you soon."

I wasn't one to sit around and wait for things to get done when a key suspect was in the wind. I got up to get my tea from the fridge and met Cassy when she grabbed her bagel from the toaster.

"Where you think she at?" Cassy asked.

"That's the million-dollar question."

"Where would you go if it was you?"

"First off, I would never kill someon—What? It's different if it's my job. And they frown on it anyway. What time do you have to be at work today?"

"Not until noon. You wanna drop me off and talk to Pumpkin Spice?"

"Yeah, I think I want to find out if Adam is back and if the drug test is done or scheduled. Is that okay? I don't want to get you in bad with the dancers," I said.

"That won' do it. It's going to take some time to get in with them anyway. Can' rush it."

****

I waited to hear from Colonel Martin, but the call never came. Sammie had gone and come back from taking the kids to daycare, and now it was time to get Cassy to work.

"You wanna go with us, Sammie? I've got errands to run once Cassy's at work. Gets you out of the house at least."

She shrugged and grabbed her bag and joined us. Since it was her dad's car, she chose to drive, even if she had to go through the city. West Saratoga was a mess this morning with construction taking up half the road. It was hit or miss until Charles Street, but then it seemed to clear up, and we were good to go.

"Your dad have any word on my car?" I asked.

"Or mine?" Cassy asked.

"He looked over Cassy's and ordered a part, but he hasn't gotten to yours yet, Laci. Uncle Randy's got him running here and yonder for parts for a bus he's trying to fix up."

"What kind of bus?" I asked. "And why?"

"Oh, who knows. I swanny my uncle has got Momma wound tighter than a clock, and she may very well tell him it's time to hit the road. This where we're going?"

She pulled into the lot in front of the Purple Pelican, and we rolled out of the car. There was a breeze in the air this morning, but all it did was spread the dumpster smell to the front of the club instead of keeping it where it belonged in the back. Cassy pulled on the door, but it didn't budge.

"Hunh, I wonder where they at," Cassy said. "I'll try around back."

I barely made out the muffled sound of my phone going off in the bottom of my bag due to the Jones Falls Expressway being basically behind us.

"Major Duval."

"Major, this is Colonel Martin. It appears that Captain and Mrs. Bishop are AWOL. I've been going rounds here with everyone, trying to find them, but no one seems to know where they went. I'll keep you informed."

She hung up before I could say anything, but the club door opened just then, and Cassy stuck her head out and waved us inside the club. Once inside I relayed my conversation to the girls, and we were all at a loss of where they could be.

"This don' look too good for them," Cassy said.

"No, no it doesn't. Let me go check on Zucca," I said.

I went to the back, and Sammie trailed behind me while Cassy went to the room for bouncers on the other side of the stage. I knocked and went in without waiting for a reply.

"Where's Luca?" I asked.

"He's on an errand for me," Zucca said. He nodded his head at us without getting out of his chair. "Good morning, Major—Mrs. Wheaton."

"You hear anything from Adam or Ted since last night?" I asked.

He leaned back in his chair and steepled his fingers against his chin with his elbows resting on the desk.

"Mr. Wilhite has not shown up to work this morning, nor have I received word that he's ended his employment here. So, I'm without a bartende—"

"I'll do that instead of bouncin' if you want, P.S." Cassy came through the door with a new black jacket in place—it swallowed her up. "This jacket don' fit anyway."

"Do you have a license, Ms. Davis?" "P.S.?" Zucca and I spoke at the same time.

"Not yet, but I can get one online for a couple hundred bucks. They make good tips, don' they? Wha's the pay compared to bouncin'? I mean, I guess I could do both if you need, just not on the same night. You know?"

"You'll have to attend an online class, take the test, and then we can proceed from there. In the meantime, you can fulfill your duties to your first position. We will figure out a schedule that suits all of us."

"Slay," Cassy said.

"Slay, girl," Sammie said.

"So, no word on Ted either, I take it?" I was so lost to the modern lingo I just pressed on. It didn't phase Zucca, though.

"None," Zucca said.

"If it's okay with you, we're utilizing Cassy's position here to keep an eye out for Ted. We want to see if the dancers know him," I said.

"My dancers are given random unscheduled drug screenings. Marijuana is not penalized, but it is frowned upon while they are performing in the club."

"Have you gotten the cameras fixed yet?" Sammie asked.

"There may still be one or two that don't perform consistently, but the rest have been updated and are monitored from the bouncer's security area."

"If you get a picture, Laci, maybe you can go through the camera footage and see if he's shown up. How long is the footage saved? Do you have it on loop recording?" Sammie asked.

"The loop is set for twenty-four hours," Zucca said. "We review before opening every shift. That will be a part of your job, Ms. Davis. If you can get me a photograph, it will make the job possible. Why the focus on Mr. Stone? Does he have something to do with your current case?"

"We're not sure yet. He's definitely a person of interest, and the fact he's missing leads me to believe he knows something."

Chapter Eighteen

"Where to?" Sammie asked.

"We're going to drop by the hospital to check on Mrs. Zimmer and see if Mr. Zimmer has a picture of Ted we can get a copy of," I said.

With Route 40 right around the corner from us, it was easy to get to Franklin Square, even if it took a little bit longer. Which was fine by me, as long as I got to stay out of the tunnels. Sammie was a good driver, and I let my mind wander while she navigated the traffic around us.

I texted Colonel Martin, asking if Ruby was still in the hospital and if she'd heard anything on Haylee yet. I got a quick reply back—yes, Ruby was still there. She gave me her room number and the fact she was under a different name. Nothing on Haylee, though.

I hit send on a text to Antonio asking him if he had any pictures of Ted when Sammie pulled into a spot in the middle of the lot. We got out and weaved our way to the front entrance, where I checked with the Information Desk—Mrs. Zimmer was still in the same room.

We stopped in the older woman's room first on the off chance I got a picture. Maybe Ruby could help me with him. I tapped and entered the room, and Mr. Zimmer was in the same chair he was in the last time I was there.

"Good morning, Mr. Zimmer," I said. "How is your wife doing?"

"She's still in her medical coma. Doctors don't know how long she'll have to stay in it. The swelling in her brain isn't coming down as quickly as they want."

"Mr. Zimmer, have you heard from your nephew since we last spoke? Do you have a picture of him by any chance? Either here or at home would work."

"Why do you people care about Ted?"

"Because he is linked to a death and two possible overdoses. I just need to ask him a few questions," I said.

"What's the link?" Mr. Zimmer crossed his arms over his chest but kept his eyes on me. He didn't reach for a phone that could hold a picture either, though. *Damnit.* "Are you calling him a suspect? I watch the shows on TV. I know subterfuge when I see it."

I did a mental head slap and pasted a smile on my face. "I would classify him more as a person of interest than I would a suspect at this point, Mr. Zimmer. This is all a technicality. I need him to clear a few things up for me."

"Ha," he barked.

I ignored Mr. Zimmer to grab my phone from my bag when it dinged. I pulled it out when I saw Antonio sent me a message with an attachment. Bingo.

"That's okay, Mr. Zimmer. I have one anyway." I flashed my phone around where he could see it, and you could tell by the way he paled that this was indeed his nephew. "I don't need you for anything else. For now."

I turned and yanked the door so hard it bounced off the wall beside me and Sammie. He'd pissed me off so much I ignored his ranting and sputtering as I left the two of them behind. Next stop would be Ruby's room.

"Now I wonder what in tarnation has him so scared that he didn't want to help," Sammie said.

"He wasn't scared, Sammie. He's protecting family."

"I think there's some of that, yes, but if you saw him while you were looking at your phone, his eyes were shifting, and he looked trapped. You only saw him once you'd gotten your picture. I tell you, he's afraid of something."

I stopped in the middle of the hallway and looked at Sammie. Maybe she was right. "Now, what would he have to be afraid of?"

"Now, how in tarnation would I know that? It's your job to figure it out—not mine. I'm only telling you what I saw when you weren't looking. Could be his wife lying in there sick as a dog because someone drugged her. That alone would frighten anyone."

We continued along the hallway to the stairs, where we went up two flights and exited onto the maternity floor, then wound our way to Ruby's room. I tapped on the door and pushed it open to see inside.

"Good morning," I said.

Ruby was sitting up in bed, and Damian sat next to her in the chair. They were holding hands, watching a talk show on TV. Damian pushed the power button when Sammie and I came in.

"I came to see how you two were doing," I said. "More importantly, how is the little Moffat doing?"

"She's doing okay." Ruby reached up and placed her hand over her stomach. "They think she's not going to show any signs of the overdose, but we won't know yet for a little while."

"Have you had any luck finding who did this?" Damian asked.

"I wanted to ask you if you know this man." I pulled up the picture Antonio sent me and placed it in Ruby's outstretched hand.

"I've never seen him before," Ruby said. "Who is he?"

"Have you, sir?" I asked.

"His face looks familiar, but I can't say where I saw him before. Does he work on Aberdeen?"

"He has family on Aberdeen, so you may have seen him there. His family actually liv—"

"That's Mrs. Zimmer's nephew." Damian snapped his fingers. "What's his name…Adam? Aidan? Something with an A."

"Ted?" I asked.

"Yes, that's it. I've seen him occasionally when he visited, but nothing recent. Why?" Damian asked.

"We just want to question him on some things. He's a person of interest in the case, but we can't seem to find him. Speaking of people we can't seem to find, have you seen or heard from Haylee or her husband?"

Ruby instantly squeezed Damian's hand on the top of the covers. It was small, but it spoke volumes.

"No." Ruby shook her head. "Why?"

"She and Dan are also missing. She was supposed to report for a polygraph test yesterday, only she never showed up."

"Why does she have to take one of those?" Ruby asked.

"She volunteered to take it," I said.

"Is she in trouble?" Damian asked.

"It doesn't look good when she skips on a polygraph, and I don't have to tell you how bad it looks when he didn't show up to work. As of right now, he's considered AWOL since he didn't report anything to his commander. So, if you know anything, it would only help them if you told me."

"Well, I'm sorry I can't help you," Ruby said. "I don't know where they are."

Ruby stopped looking me in the eyes, and Damian only had eyes for his wife.

"Well, I'm glad you and the baby are okay. I'll check on you in a couple of days. In the meantime, if you hear from either of them, I'd appreciate it if you'd let me or Colonel Martin know."

Once outside her door, I dialed Colonel Martin. Ruby and Damian knew where Haylee was—I knew it like I knew my own name.

"Colonel, I'm visiting Ruby and Damian. They know where Haylee and her husband are," I said. "And no, they didn't tell me."

"Then all we can do is wait," she said.

"Yes, ma'am. I'm going to hang out here for a bit and see if I can catch them coming to see Ruby and Damian. I'll keep you informed." I turned to Sammie and glanced at my watch. "You're good if we wait here a bit? Are you hungry? You want to go grab a bite?"

While Sammie went in search of the cafeteria and sweet tea, I went in search of the nurse in charge of the maternity floor and explained why she would be seeing a lot of me today. She gave me permission to sit in the nurse's area so I wouldn't be spotted from the elevators. I couldn't play on my phone since I needed to be on alert for visitors to Ruby's room.

It was a long afternoon. Sammie came and brought more sweet tea and a sandwich, so I didn't have to leave the area. Then, when nature called due to all the tea, she manned my spot so I wouldn't miss anything. She then decided to go check on the cars and her Uncle Randy at her dad's house and would come and pick me up later. When she called to let me know she'd have to go get the twins since it was later than she planned, I took that as a sign and messaged Rev to see if he'd be able to come and get me. He gave me a thumbs-up emoji, which I took to mean we were good to go.

I noticed there were plenty of people going in and out of Ruby's room. Some with equipment and some with clipboards, but none looked like Haylee in disguise. No sooner did that idea cross my mind than the food people came to serve dinner, but while they parked the trolley outside her door, no one went in, but the door opened, and no one came out.

"Can you call for security for me? Now?" I was immediately on my feet and on my way to their room. "I need them to room 606, please. STAT." I always wanted to say that.

I pushed my way inside without knocking and interrupted Haylee mid-sentence. Her shoulders dropped, and her mouth snapped shut.

"Major," she said.

"Mrs. Bishop," I said. "I would ask what you're doing here and not at the sheriff's office taking your polygraph, but I can guess."

"You don't understand," Haylee said.

"Then explain." I leaned my back against the door so anyone coming in would have to go through me.

"I know I'm your number one suspect, but I didn't

do it. I knew you were closing in on me, and I couldn't take that chance."

"So, you decided to run? You realize that's the first sign of a guilty person, right?"

"That's not just on the TV?" she asked.

What was it with people getting all their police knowledge off the television?

"No, that's real life, Haylee," I said.

"But she didn't do it," Ruby said.

"Well, then it's up to her—Oh, here they are." I opened the door and let the security guard in. "Mrs. Bishop, I'm sorry, but I'm going to have to take you in for questioning. Running was the wrong thing to do. Where is your husband? Aberdeen is looking for him since he's AWOL."

"AWOL? But why? Where is he?" Haylee's eyes were wide open, and I think it finally sank in just how deep of trouble she was in.

"Because he is absent without leave. He's a no-show, and now the entire post is on alert looking for him. It really would have been easier if you'd just come in for your polygraph, but now we have to do it the hard way.

"Gentlemen—" I said.

"No!" Ruby yelled from the bed. "You can't arrest her. You can't."

"That's not your decision, Mrs. Moffat. Time to go."

The security guards and I ushered her out the door, and you could hear Ruby crying inside. These were the moments it sucked doing my job, but when it came down to it, someone was still dead, and it was my job to find who did it.

I texted Rev that we were on our way to the front of the hospital if he could be there ASAP. He said he was right around the corner and would be there in two.

We reached the lobby, and the security guards left me with Haylee. She was quietly crying and wiping her tears with the sleeve of her T-shirt.

"Where are we going now?" she asked.

"We're going to the sheriff's office to get the polygraph done. Once we get there, you can call your husband or the Army Trial Defense Services you were assigned."

"Why are you doing this?" she asked.

"Because someone's dead."

Rev pulled up just then, so we didn't get to speak anymore. I put her up front with him so I could keep an eye on her and called Deputy Robinson and Colonel Martin once we were on our way. Colonel Martin said she would meet me there. I told Rev to take it slow so we wouldn't upset Haylee any further and to give Colonel Martin time to get there.

For a second, when we reached the light at the corner of Mountain Road and Pulaski, I feared she might run for it, but instead, she gave an *urk* when Rev stepped on the gas to pass someone while in the right lane. There were horns and fingers flying from the driver's seat, but Haylee seemed to be somewhere else. I needed to remind myself why Haylee was a suspect in the first place. I couldn't let my guard down for a second.

Colonel Martin opened the car door for Haylee when we arrived, and we all proceeded into the sheriff's office. Colonel Martin gave Rev the side-eye—I forgot this was her first time seeing him. I was introducing her to lots of new people these days. The only ones she hadn't met were Zucca and Luca. She would probably never speak to me again once this was all finished.

"Good afternoon, Deputy Robinson. This is an associate, Colonel Martin. Colonel Martin is in charge of the Army Criminal Investigation Division at Aberdeen. She's been kind enough to let me help her with this case."

That got me the side-eye from Colonel Martin, and I bit back a smile.

"Okay," he said. "Are you staying while we do the test?"

"I think we'll sit in the conference room if that's okay with you. I told Mrs. Bishop she gets her phone calls if you could help her out. We'll be here when you finish and go from there."

Colonel Martin and I made our way to the conference room from the other day, and Rev left to go to the grocery store around the corner. He told me he'd be back to get me when I called.

"You know lots of colorful people," Colonel Martin said.

"Yeah, my world expanded when I came home again," I said.

"Oh, wait, you're from here?" she asked.

I went through my history and touched on Antonio a little bit. She had lots of questions about him, but I tried to preserve some of my dignity. Ultimately, the truth came out, and I admitted how I'd messed up.

"Colonel Ellis and I have a history," she said. My mouth fell open.

"Wait. You do, too?" I asked.

"What do you mean, too?" she asked.

I filled her in on our deployment from ten years ago and how it came after Zach and I divorced, but nothing ever came of it.

"Once I saw him here, he let it be known he would be more than happy to pick up where we left off, but I just can't."

"Wow," she said. "At least you didn't find yourself leaving him at the altar."

I must have had Cassy's chair from the other day because suddenly, my chair sprang back, and Colonel Martin grabbed my flailing arms to help me right myself.

"You're the 'one that got away,' " I said.

"Is that what he said?" I nodded, and she went on. "It was about five years ago. When he walked into the room the other day, you could have knocked me over with a feather. I haven't seen him since before the wedding. It wasn't my proudest moment, but I don't regret it."

"I'm so sorry," I said. "What a pair we are. You leave one at the altar, and I leave one to marry an idiot." We busted out laughing, and it was then that Deputy Robinson came into the room. "How'd it go, Robinson?"

"I don't know. We haven't started yet. Isn't she here with you?"

"Laci—" Rev spoke from behind Robinson outside the door. "That girl is trying to take off with my car. I figured you'd want to know."

We raced from the room and down the hallway, where Colonel Martin and I burst through the front door. Haylee wasn't at Rev's car, but neither was she where we could see her either.

"There are houses on the other side of these woods. We might want to try there first," Deputy Robinson said.

"We'll go through the woods if you want to drive around to the other side, Deputy," Colonel Martin said.

"Rev, would you mind staying here in case we missed her and she's watching us from somewhere? The volume is up on my phone."

"I've got a few men watching for her," Robinson said.

While Colonel Martin was dressed in OCPs and combat boots, I hadn't dressed for literal field work that day. My tennis shoes would have to do, and I could only pray the mosquitoes liked her better than they did me.

We waded into the woods, and I debated calling for Haylee, but I didn't want to tip her off on our whereabouts. Colonel Martin was equally as silent. The woods were thick, and we couldn't see out the other side yet. I separated myself from Colonel Martin but kept her in my line of sight. It was eerily quiet—even the traffic noise died off, and we were only seventy-five yards from Route 40. I'd hate to be here at night.

After about thirty minutes in the woods, I was beginning to feel like Moses. It was then that Deputy Robinson met up with us in the middle.

"Nothing came out the other side," he said. He turned around, and we followed him out of the woods. "You want a ride back to the office?"

We agreed, and it was while he was making a U-turn out of the apartment complex when I saw her.

"There she is—" Colonel Martin pointed to Pulaski, where a woman was running for a car parked at the curb.

Deputy Robinson flicked on the lights, and we were off and running. I texted Rev that we were tracking her down so he could go home if need be. Instead, he said he would help. I tried to get him to leave it alone, but he was a man on a mission.

At the light by the sheriff's office, Rev pulled out and sideswiped the car carrying Haylee. I didn't know who was driving the getaway car, but they managed to get it back on the road and around Rev. This didn't deter Rev, but he must have floored it—all that was left was his dust.

Now, Deputy Robinson was no slouch in the speed department, but there was no catching Haylee's car, let alone Rev. Colonel Martin and I could only hang on while we raced down Pulaski Highway in hot pursuit of Haylee.

Chapter Nineteen

"Now, why would she run?" Colonel Martin asked.

"I honestly don't know," I said. "She insists she's innocent but then goes and pulls a stunt like this. It's like she's begging to be arrested and shut away for years."

"Where did you find the big guy? Rev, is it?" Colonel Martin asked.

"I called his company, Revved, for a ride once, and he's been with us since. He has a lead foot, though."

"No kidding." Deputy Robinson spoke from the front seat.

"He's been on his best behavior, sir. Besides, right now, he seems to be doing a good job of keeping up with Haylee."

We were out of Edgewood and approaching Riverside. We'd passed the infamous billboard which now sported an advertisement for WJZ. *Sigh.* I missed Bob Turk.

"Wait, what happened to Bata Shoes?" I swiveled my head to look for the old shoe factory that was a part of my childhood.

"They tore it down," Robinson said. "Back in the 2000s. They wanted to develop the waterfront."

I guess the less said about that, the better. It didn't sound like Robinson liked it very much, and I can't say I blamed him. What a bummer.

Right when we got to the intersection of Pulaski and Route 543, Haylee's car took a last-minute turn to the onramp of 543. They cut across three lanes of traffic, but the only one to suffer was Rev, who flew past them and kept going down Route 40.

Robinson made the quick turn, and we got within three cars of them when they started weaving in and out of traffic. They would be lucky if they got out of this with their car intact. Even with the lights and siren, people just couldn't move out of the way fast enough.

It was at the light at Church Creek Road and 543 that Haylee's luck ran out. The light was red, and they were ready to run it when a pedestrian began crossing from Crêpe Magic, a local breakfast place on the right corner, to the gas station across the parkway. The driver slammed on the brakes and swerved to miss them and ended up in the parking lot of Crêpe Magic but left the entire underside of their car in the grassy embankment they bottomed out then flew over. It was like the opening scene of that old '70s TV show when they flew through the air, only there was no *yeehaww*. I imagined there was lots of grunting, though.

Robinson took a right on what felt like two wheels and then swung the SUV to the left to get to them in the parking lot before they escaped. He needn't have worried, because Haylee was flat on her face when we got to her. The driver, however, was gone. A brief look over the top of the car, and I saw him bounce off the front right fender of Rev's car.

I ran after him and met Rev after he yanked the emergency brake inside and got out to check what he hit. Rev grabbed a hold of the back of his shirt—but he was struggling to break free.

"Well, hello there," I said.

"Fu—"

"Hey." Rev shook him by the collar. It didn't take a genius to realize he was not going to say hello.

"It doesn't matter anyhow," I said. "Pretty sure you're going to be seeing the inside of a cell for the immediate futu—"

Despite Rev's grip on him, the guy tore off his shirt and ran. Oh, it was on now. I took off after him down Church Camp Road behind the strip mall. I mean, really—where the hell did he think he was going? I could hear the sound of running feet behind me, but I didn't dare take my eyes off of him.

Up ahead, there was a small break in the fence, which ran along the back of the strip mall, and he aimed right for it. I turned up the gas and cleared it seconds behind him. Colonel Martin caught up to me then, and we were neck and neck in who would reach him first at that point.

Then he made his big mistake. He turned down the first road he got to and didn't realize it was a dead end in the form of a small residential area. Out of the corner of my eye, Colonel Martin ran to our right and disappeared behind a small house into the wooded backyard. I kept the guy in sight, and he slowed down when he reached the driveway to the house. Once he located which side he was going to run through, he took off, but I was close now.

No sooner did he cut through the small carport than the side door of the house came open, and I yelled for them to get back inside. The old guy didn't like that, and he tried to grab my arm, but I sidestepped him. He threw me off stride, and I lost the man I was chasing. I slid to a stop at the end of the carport in time to see a beautiful sight.

Colonel Martin leapt over the plastic Adirondack chairs placed around a firepit and tackled the guy we were chasing. They both landed with an *oof* on one of the chairs on the other side. It tipped over, and he tried to take off again, but she lashed out with her right foot and swift-kicked him in the right knee. He went down with a scream—reminded me of my recent experience with that same maneuver.

I came up beside them, and the owner of the house hobbled to the end of the carport, yelling at us that he was going to call the police.

"You do that," I said. "Tell them you have special agents in your backyard, and they've apprehended a suspect."

"You're what?" he asked.

"Never mind, I'll do it." I yanked my phone out of my sports bra and called Robinson.

"On your feet," Colonel Martin said.

"You have a lot to answer for, Mr. Stone."

Colonel Martin whipped her head around at me and then at the guy on the ground. He was grasping his knee, but he heard me, and he knew he was caught.

****

Once we were settled into Rev's car and following Deputy Robinson while he transported Haylee and Ted to Bel Air and the Harford County Detention Center, we were finally able to catch our collective breaths. They were on their way to be processed and would get the chance to call for an attorney. We didn't need to keep up with Deputy Robinson—they would be processed before we could get our questions answered.

"How did you know it was him?" Rev asked.

"Desio sent me a picture," I said. "I still don't understand how they know each other or the link, but hopefully, that's something we'll find out soon. I'm hoping one will squeal on the other, to be honest. Are you okay, Colonel Martin?"

"Oh yes, I'm fine. It's been a while since I've run like that. I may need to step up my workout routine if this keeps up."

"So, Haylee didn't have anything to say?" I asked.

"She clammed up when the sheriff questioned her while you two were chasing down the dude," Rev said. "She chipped her front tooth, too. Looks like it musta hurt. How old are you two anyway?"

"Well, that's random," Colonel Martin said. "I'm forty-seven. Why?"

"I'm forty-three. Didn't we just have this conversation?" I asked.

"I just wanted to say how impressed I am that you two could run like that. You could run circles around men half your age. Hell—you just did. And then he comes back limping? Which one of you did it?"

Colonel Martin and I spoke at the same time. "I'm not telling." "I don't know what you're talking about."

"Yeah, right." Rev tipped his head back and laughed. The level rivaled Cassy's. "You guys hungry?"

We agreed we could eat, so we parked it in front of Groov's and got out to grab some chicken. Personally, I needed to move before the aches settled in, but I couldn't tell if Colonel Martin was feeling the same or not. *Oop*—yep—she was. I pretended I didn't see her hunch her back and stretch it when we got out.

"Just what I need," I said. "A tall, sweet tea with lots and lots of sugar and grease in the form of chicken."

"How the hell you drink tea this late and get to sleep on time?" Colonel Martin asked.

"How the hell you know that word?" I asked.

"Will you two quit cussing like sailors and get in here so I can order?" Rev held the door open, and the irony of his statement was not lost on us. We all laughed, and I know my sides hurt when I finished.

I answered my phone when I reached my table. The little number card was propped on the edge where it could be seen—this was my treat. Colonel Martin was in the bathroom and Rev was filling his cup up with soda. It was Cassy. See, I looked every once in a while before I answered.

"Yep?" I answered.

"You done actually looked this time?" Cassy said.

"Oh, hush, what do you want?"

"Where you at?"

"We're at Groov's in Bel Air, and boy, do I have a story to tell you. Wait, didn't you check the app I put on your phone?"

"Where's it at? I think I mighta deleted it. Anyways, can you come get me from work? I can' get Sammie nowhere."

"We're in Bel Air waiting to get to Haylee and Ted. I'll call Robinson and see how long he thinks it's going to be. Can't you get a ride from P.S.?"

"You figured it out, hunh? He had lots to say 'bout that once you was gone. I done told him I'm not changin' it. We'll see who breaks first. All right. Let me know."

I hung up, then called Robinson to see what the timetable looked like. He reported it was still going to be at least another hour. They would need to contact a lawyer. Without Haylee's husband in the picture, they couldn't use the Army legal counsel.

"Has Haylee mentioned where Dan is?" I asked.

"Not to me she hasn't," Deputy Robinson said. "She called Mr. Stone to come pick her up in Edgewood. That much I was able to get from her."

I texted Cassy to let her know we would come and get her. It looked like Colonel Martin would get to come along for the ride—I put her up front with Rev, and he did not disappoint. There was honking and cussing, and hands and fingers thrown all over the place on the ride to get Cassy.

"Did you say you used to be a preacher?" Colonel Martin pried her fingers off the armrest on her door. The handle above the window was long gone.

"Yeah, turns out I don't have the patience for people like I used to."

"No kidding," Colonel Martin said.

"This way, I get to do what I want and meet who I want. Look at me now. I get to meet a woman with fancy-ass birds sewn on her."

I tried, really I did, but I couldn't help it. The fact that he reduced a full bird colonel to someone with a "fancy-ass bird sewn on her" was too much—even for me. I doubled over in the back seat, laughter poured out of me. Colonel Martin put up a good fight, but eventually, she gave in and laughed until she snorted. Rev looked confused.

"Rev," I gasped. "Rev, Colonel Martin is as high up as you can go before becoming a general. Show some respect."

"It's okay." Colonel Martin wiped a tear from her eye. "It keeps me humble. How far are we going to get this person?"

"It's my roomy, Cassy. She's a bouncer in the city. You met her before an interview sometime." I cut off to answer my phone for Sammie. "Hiya, Sammie, what's up?"

"Do you know what Cassy wanted? I tried to call her back, but she didn't pick up."

"She was probably talking to me. We're on our way to pick her up from the club. Any word on our cars?"

"Cassy's is all set. Next up is yours. Momma threw Uncle Randy out. He's staying at a local motel for the time being—if that don't beat all. I swanny I don't know why he doesn't just go home. I'm sure Aunt Tiffy is enjoying her peace, but enough is enough already. He's got to go."

"Where is Aunt Tiffy?" I asked.

Colonel Martin swiveled her head to me in the back, and I held up a finger. Rev was colorfully addressing the drivers we passed on 95, and I held onto the bar above my window for dear life—at least mine was still there.

"Aunt Tiffy is in Knoxville. Or rather, a small town called Strawberry Plains. We just say, Knox—"

"Sammie." I interrupted her. "Did you need anything else?"

"Nah, I'm okay. Is that Rev, I hear? Tell him Ryan's been asking about him again. If someone told me Ry would get attached to—Oops, here I go again. I'll see y'all later. Bye."

She hung up, and I stared at my phone. It was the sudden braking under the train bridge that grabbed my attention. Colonel Martin braced herself on the dash, but my head bounced off the back of her seat.

"What the hell, Rev?"

"It's not me, hon. It's these city drivers. They're crazy."

With a jerk of the wheel, we took the right for East Monument Street, and before I knew it, we were passing the Coca-Cola Bottling Company on our right. Once on Madison, we would pass Johns Hopkins. I may not come this way often, but even I knew where Hopkins was.

With a left on Holiday, we ran under the Jones Falls Expressway and finally emerged beside the club with Rev turning into the parking lot. I texted Cassy we were there, then sat back and waited for her to come out.

—*P.S. wants to speak whichu.*— Cassy texted. —*Come through the back.*—

"Damnit," I said. "Colonel Martin, you want to go meet Zucca? Rev, you've met him already."

"Zucca?" she asked.

"You'll see," I said.

We entered through the rear entrance, which was different for me. The back hallway in the club held the dressing rooms for the dancers in addition to the security room for the bouncers. It was completely dark when we stepped inside, but after a second or two, my eyes adjusted, and we pushed forward to the door of the inner club. I called for Cassy, and she stuck her head out of Zucca's office and waved me over.

"Howdy, Colonel," Cassy said.

Pamela Kyel

Colonel Martin nodded at Cassy while doing a thorough look around the club. It wasn't in the worst category of clubs I'd seen, but then it wasn't in the best either. When we reached Zucca's door, I passed through in front of Colonel Martin and greeted him at his desk. Luca wasn't there.

"Is she fired already?" He looked slightly startled at my question, but then he realized I was joking when he saw my grin. His eyes swept past me and landed on Colonel Martin. "Oh, let me introduce you to Colonel Martin. Colonel Martin, this is Mr. Zucca. He's, uh, a local business owner I met when looking for my ex-husband's murderer last month. Zucca, this is Colonel Martin. She's in charge of the Army Criminal Investigation Division at Aberdeen. Basically, the Army version of OSI."

He stood up and stretched out his hand to shake hers. Colonel Martin was silent when her hand met his, but I'd never seen him stand up for anyone before.

"Welcome, Colonel," Zucca said. "It's an honor."

"Oh. Thank you."

"What did you need to see me for, Zucca?" I asked.

"Adam Wilhite is doubling down on his lack of appearance while simultaneously putting pressure on me to drop his drug test. I no longer doubt he is imbibing some sort of substance he obtained from Mr. Stone. Where is Mr. Stone? Cassy told me you have him. I must speak with him."

"I don't have him," I said. "Cassy, you know I don't have him. He's being booked into the Harford County Detention Center. We're on our way there now to question him. You're welcome to come al—"

"Yes, I'll do that. I have my own transportation. I

216

will just be a moment."

He strode from the room and went into the closet Antonio and I hid in. I didn't know if we were supposed to wait or not, but before we decided one way or the other, he was back out. He switched the light off inside before he came out—I had no idea there was a switch in there anywhere.

We followed him out the back door and met up with Rev and Luca outside. They were deep in conversation but stopped abruptly when we stepped outside.

"Luca, we are off to Bel Air, God help me," Zucca said. He put his sunglasses on and approached the large black SUV that wasn't there when we pulled up. "Colonel Martin, would you be so kind as to keep me company for the drive?"

"Wait a sec—"

"Sure," she said.

She went to the right, where the SUV was parked, and I stopped in my tracks. Cassy slammed into the back of me, which propelled me into Rev's car, and I threw up my hands to avoid crashing into the passenger door.

"Now ain' that interestin'," Cassy said.

"Yes. Yes, it is," I said.

Chapter Twenty

I took the drive in silence, only half paying attention to what Cassy said from the back. Not because I cared one way or the other about Colonel Martin and Zucca but because the world was once again whizzing by my window. Despite having just driven down Madison to get to the club, it was now shut down. There was some sort of accident, and everyone was being rerouted from Holiday. Rev knew we needed to get to Bel Air, and the easiest way was 95, which meant the Fort McHenry Tunnel. Oh, joy. I didn't always get nervous driving through it, but today just happened to be my lucky day.

"How's Amaré?" I desperately tried to get my mind off of what was coming.

"He's fine. Busy studying for his promotion."

"What's the next step for him?" I asked.

"Detective. Said he wants to work with Desio more closely. I done told him he better do it sooner rather than later then."

"Why sooner rather than later?" I asked.

"Sometimes I get the feeling Desio don' want to keep doin' this. You know what I'm sayin'?"

"I think we all feel that way at some point. I can't really picture him doing anything else, though."

"You can' picture him as your pool boy?" Cassy asked. I turned, and she tried to present a mask of innocence, but I knew better.

"No, I don't picture him as my pool boy," I said.

"Only 'cause you ain' gotta pool." She thought that was funny and threw her head back and laughed her boisterous laugh. I huffed out a laugh and turned back to the front.

We took the rest of the drive in silence, and what would normally be a forty-five-minute drive turned into thirty-two, and that was *with* the route change. When we pulled into the lot for visitors, it looked like there were a bunch of people already there for something. It wasn't until I heard Cassy's "Uh-oh" that I knew something was up.

"What's going on?" Rev asked.

"Looks like they spillin' tea over there," Cassy said.

"Tea?" I asked. "Sweet tea?"

Cassy laughed. "Naw, this kinda tea is the talkin' kind. They gathered 'round yakkin' 'bout something' over there. Uh-oh. Don' look, Laci. You ain' gonna like this."

"What?" My nose smacked the window while I tried to figure out what she was talking about. Then I saw him.

"What the absolute hell is Desio doing here?" I was out the door the second Rev put the car in park. Once out, I realized he wasn't the only outlier there, I said, "What the hell are you doing here, Wesley?"

She pushed her chin up and crossed her arms over her chest. I got within inches of her, and I was seeing red.

"Don', Laci. Waters done told you to leave her alone." Cassy said.

Cassy was right, but I was beyond angry. I may not be able to lash out at her, but I could at Desio. "Why are you here, Desio? This is outside of your jurisdiction." I glanced behind him and there were more monkeys in this circus than I could count. "Colonel Waters? Kristen? What on earth is going on here?" I sidestepped Desio. If he wanted to be there, it would be without me—he and Wesley could…I wasn't going to finish that thought.

Before I got to Colonel Waters, I looked around the parking lot at the others. Asher was speaking to Colonel Martin, or rather at her; she didn't look like she cared what he said. Zucca stood behind them, chatting with Luca to his right—he kept an eye on Asher.

Entering the picture from the parked car beside this group emerged Dan Bishop and his counsel. Dan was in sweats and sported a ballcap—there were no cuffs.

"What's going on, sir?" I asked Colonel Waters again.

"Maple sausage, Major. I was requested to get down here by Lieutenant Colonel Ellis. He informed me there would be questioning at the Detention Center and we should be there. Then I get here, and it's worse than a three-ringed circus. I don't know what the hell is going on. I don't know why I'm here. I don't know why any of us are here. Do you?"

"No, sir," I said, "but I'm going to go find out."

I bypassed Desio and ignored Wesley and stepped right in front of Asher. I interrupted whatever line he was feeding Colonel Martin.

"Why are these people here, Asher?" I asked.

"You will address me as Colonel Ellis, Major," Asher said.

I reared back in surprise. Where did that come from?

"Yes, *Asher*," Colonel Martin said. "Why are all these people here?"

He didn't like her calling him that because he suddenly looked like he'd sucked a lemon. But there wasn't anything he could do about it. She outranked him—it was glorious.

"Colonel Martin," he said through gritted teeth. "These people are here because they all have something to do with the investigation."

"She doesn't." Colonel Martin pointed at Wesley. "Didn't we ask you once to stay away? You don't belong here. You will not be let in. Next? Colonel Waters? I thought you turned the investigation over to Major Duvall here. Do you doubt her ability to solve it?"

"I do not," he said. "I don't want to be here. I don't need to be here. Good-bye."

Colonel Martin proceeded through the remaining people and sent those home who didn't belong. When she finished, Wesley was still there.

"Why are you still here?" Colonel Martin asked.

"This is my investigation, too," she said.

"I disagree, and as the one in charge, I tell you it's time for you to go. I would also consider a career change if I were you. Asher, take this one and leave." Colonel Martin turned her back on her, and that was that. "Major, I believe that's all of us."

"Have you got it figured out yet?" Deputy Robinson stormed down the sidewalk from the front of the Detention Center.

"I believe so," Colonel Martin said. "There will

be—how many of us are there now?"

"Six," I said.

Colonel Martin, Cassy, Dan and his counsel, Zucca, and I followed Deputy Robinson into the Interagency Processing Center, where there was a room set up for us to use. With a glance at all the uniforms around us, Zucca decided that an observation room would be more to his liking. He stepped behind the glass window with Cassy. Rev decided it was too crowded and would come back for us later.

"There was no bail set, considering we spent most of the day chasing Mrs. Bishop and Mr. Stone down," Robinson said. "We'll bring them in one at a time. You can sit on this side of the table."

"You're taking the ball on this one, Major," Colonel Martin said.

"You're sure, ma'am?" I asked. "How about if any of us have any questions for Haylee, we can say them if there's an opening? Dan, I'm sorry you have to be here like this. Hello again, Major Barnes. Are you prepared with questions?"

"I'm not prepared for any of this," Major Barnes said.

"Dan, did you know where Haylee was today? How does she know Ted?" I asked.

"My client is not the one being questioned today," Major Barnes said.

"I realize that, Major, but there are things he could tell us that would cut down on things we have to ask Haylee," I said.

"I didn't know where she was. I knew she was with Ted. They're related," Dan said. "I spoke with her this morning, but that was it."

"Did she tell you she would be skipping out on the polygraph?" I asked.

"No," Dan said. "I thought that's where she was going."

"Where have you been all day then?" I asked.

"That's irrelevant, Major," Major Barnes said. "He is addressing it with General Fields separately."

The door to the room opened then, and Deputy Robinson guided Haylee into the room. She was already in the center's uniform, and her hands were cuffed in front of her. Dan stared at her—his hands were clenched white on the table in front of him. Once she was seated, Deputy Robinson took his place in the chair next to Colonel Martin.

"Are you sure you want to do this without counsel present?" Major Barnes asked.

"I do," Haylee said.

"Can you tell us why you ran away, Haylee?" I asked.

"Because I know who killed Jill," Haylee said.

"You do?" I asked. "Would you care to tell me who it is?"

"It's Mrs. Zimmer," she said.

"Mrs. Zimmer? How do you know that? What evidence do you have?" I asked.

"She pushed Ruby into taking the anxiety medicine. Ruby told me she didn't want to, but Mrs. Zimmer insisted."

"But Mrs. Zimmer herself is in the hospital now because of a drug overdose. Are you saying she also drugged herself?" Colonel Martin asked.

"Yes, that's what I'm saying. I know it doesn't make any sense, but Te—"

"What is Ted to you?" I asked.

"Ted is my cousin on my dad's side," she said. "My dad is his mother's brother."

"So, how are the Zimmers related to you?" I asked.

"They're not," she said. "The Zimmers are related to Ted's birth father, but he died a long time ago."

My head was spinning from trying to picture the family tree. It sounded like the Zimmers were distant and only related through marriage, not by blood.

"What proof do you have that Mrs. Zimmer killed Jill?" Colonel Martin asked. "You only mentioned her poisoning herself and Ruby but nothing about her and Jill."

"Ted told me. He told me Jill was blackmailing Mrs. Zimmer about something. He wouldn't tell me what, though."

"How can you take Ted's word for it?" I asked.

"Because he's family," she said.

"One thing I don't get," Colonel Martin said. "What did Ted do with the medicine bottles from the overdoses? Why did he take them? Where are they?"

"I think we need to question Ted," I said. "Robinson?"

Deputy Robinson got up and left to get Ted for us to question.

"Why do you have to question him?" Haylee asked. "I just answered your questions."

"Why are you protecting him?" I asked. "Hasn't he gotten you in enough trouble?"

"He didn't do anything I didn't ask for." She turned to Dan. "I'm sorry, Danny. I know you warned me about him. I'm sorry I didn't listen. But he's my only cousin. I had to help."

"Yeah, and look where it got you," Dan said.

"Mrs. Bishop, I can help you, but you have to want to be helped," Major Barnes said.

"How can you help?" I asked.

"I know lawyers in the area, and they would be here if I asked them."

"You might wanna call and get them here," I said. "She's not going to ask. She's going to go down with her cousin if I'm guessing right."

Major Barnes followed Deputy Robinson from the room. He held his phone in his hand and was dialing already. We sat around the room in quiet. I didn't know what else to ask Haylee. Her cousin had such an emotional stranglehold on her no one could get through.

The door opened, and a man in uniform entered the room for Haylee. "I don't want to go," Haylee cried. "Dan?" He took her elbow and guided her from the room. We heard her crying after he shut the door. Dan buried his face in his hands.

Less than a minute later, Deputy Robinson rejoined us, and he had Ted with him. The last to enter was Mr. Vass, and I sucked in my breath when I saw him. I must have sucked in too hard because now all I could do was cough. I couldn't seem to stop. It's a small world when I see the same lawyer who represented a client on the last case I had for the Air Force.

"What's wrong with you?" Colonel Martin asked.

I waved my hand in front of my face and swallowed a couple times. "Ted, we've just learned about your relation to Haylee. Can you tell me your relation to the Zimmers?" I asked.

Ted glanced at Mr. Vass before answering. "They're my great-aunt and uncle on my dad's side."

"How do you know Jill Westfall?" I asked.

"She was my aunt and uncle's neighbor," he said.

"Is that all you know about her?" Colonel Martin asked.

"She was part of some club." He shrugged and kept his head bowed.

"How old are you?" I asked.

"Why?" he asked.

"Just curious," I said. "How long have you been an EMT?"

"Been doin' it a few years. Since before I got out of high school," he said. In Maryland, you can begin the process in high school if you have a parent or guardian sign off on it.

"How long have you been dealing?" I asked.

"Who says he's dealing?" Mr. Vass asked.

"A local businessman whose worker bought from your client," I said. "I'm merely establishing a history here, Mr. Vass. What's the procedure for drugs when it's an overdose?" I asked.

"W—"

"Why are you asking that?" Mr. Vass asked.

"Because your client has been at the scene of at least two overdoses that I know of, and in both instances, it was reported that he took the medication with him when he left. I just want to know if that's normal."

"No, we're supposed to turn everything in to the police when they get there."

"Did you turn yours in to the police?" I already knew the answer, but I wanted to see what he would say. He didn't answer, which I guess is better than lying outright. "What did you do with it?"

"I didn't eat the drugs, if that's what you're asking. I wouldn't do that," he said.

"That's not what I'm asking at all. I'm asking what you did with the drugs after two overdoses. I'd also like to know how it is you answered the call to these houses and these people. Your aunt? Your aunt's neighbor? Did you know these were going to occur, and you volunteered to work? You know I can find out, right?"

He didn't say anything.

"Why did you drag Mrs. Bishop into this?" Colonel Martin asked.

"I didn't drag her," he said. "She insisted on coming. She said she was trying to save me. Whatever that means."

"It means she cared about you enough to try and keep you out of whatever trouble you were getting yourself into." Dan exploded into speech beside me. "But you didn't care, did you? You've never cared about anyone other than yourself. Haylee wouldn't be in here if it weren't for you. Why did you come back? Why didn't you just stay gone? You were supposed to."

"Come back from where?" I asked.

"Rehab," Ted mumbled. "They tricked me into rehab six months ago. My aunt and uncle drove me up and dropped me off and ran as fast as they could."

"Is that why you gave your aunt the drugs? Enough to overdose and kill her? Were you mad that she made you go to rehab?" I asked.

"She's dead?" he whispered. "I didn't—I can't—"

"Not yet," I said. "She's in a medically induced coma to try and save her life. A life you tried to end."

"That's enough," Mr. Vass said. "We're done here."

"That's fine," I said. "I think we got everything we needed. We'll be in touch with charges."

Chapter Twenty-One

"Did he admit to poisoning those people?" Cassy asked.

"Nope," I said. "Mr. Vass knows it, too. So, we have to find proof that he knew the poison was in there and took it to cover his aunt if Haylee is to be believed."

"Why would the ol' woman poison them and herself?" Cassy asked.

"Maybe she's covering for someone," Rev said.

"Don't think I haven't thought that, Rev, but who?" I asked.

"Who all the players here?" Cassy asked.

"Jill is dead. Ruby and Mrs. Zimmer are in the hospital due to overdose. That reminds me—I need to make sure the sheriff sends someone to Mrs. Zimmer. I don't want her high-tailing it out once she's better.

"I don' think she goin' anywhere anytime soon," Cassy said.

We were on our way home from Bel Air, and I opened my phone, ready to dial, when it went off. I didn't recognize the number, but that's not news. With my job, people I didn't know called me all the time. I was a scammer's dream.

"Major Duvall," I said.

"Major, this is Major Katz. I'm calling as the Investigative Officer for your open investigation. Is now a good time?"

"I'm sorry, Major who? Major Cats?"

"Katz, ma'am. Spelled K-A-T-Z," he said.

"Oh, sorry, Major. And no, now is not a good time. Do you need to see me in person, or will this be done over the phone?"

"We can take care of everything over the phone and email. If we do it through video, you won't need to have your statement sworn—so less steps."

"Can you give me about three hours? I'm in the middle of an investigation, and time is of the essence."

"Yes, ma'am; I can do that. Would you like to video or telephone? Will eight o'clock this evening be convenient?"

"Eight o'clock tonight on the telephone is fine, Major. Email me the steps for getting my statement sworn, though. You can reach me at this number again. If I don't answer, it's because I've had a break in the case."

"Yes, ma'am. I'll try later. Goodbye."

He hung up, and for a second, I was tempted to heave my phone out the window, but I didn't do it. Instead, I banged it against my forehead.

"You all right there?" Rev asked.

"I'm fine," I said.

"Was that the investigation into you?" Cassy asked.

"Yeah. He'll call back later and do the interview. I'd actually forgotten about it. I almost yeeted my phone because I don't—what?"

Cassy couldn't answer because she couldn't catch her breath. She was in a fit of laughter, and I had a feeling it was due to something I said. I thought back over it, but for the life of me, I had no idea where I went wrong.

"You said, 'yeet.' " And she was off again.

"Did I use it wrong?" I asked.

"Yeah, but only 'cause no one uses that no more. You showin' your age."

"Oh, good grief. I'm not that much older than you are."

"You got me by ten, Laci, and in that comment alone, it shows."

I showed her what I thought of that, and she roared again. Even Rev chuckled. I would have too, if I hadn't felt like crying instead.

****

The house was quiet when I stepped inside. Cassy grabbed a ride with Rev to Sammie's dad's house to get her car. It would be nice to have two forms of transportation immediately available for once. Sammie was out picking up the kids from day care, so I had the place to myself for a few minutes. If only I didn't have a cloud hanging over my head.

I opened the back door, and Needles flew through the hanging screen on his way to freedom. I hiked up the stairs to jump in the shower while I could enjoy the quiet.

I was honestly surprised at how I'd adjusted to the noise and chaos of a house full of people in the last month. It wasn't until moments like this when I remembered what it was like to be alone. Sure, I missed the silence and solitude sometimes. I'm sure everyone would clear out if I asked, but in all honesty, I loved having a full house as much as I loved the family we made together. That was one thing about life in the military—when you weren't around your immediate family, you found ways to create one.

I jumped out after the water started to cool, but I didn't go very far because I joined Boo on the bed. This day had been a tough one, and it wasn't over yet. I wasn't one to cry, but as I lay there, I felt some tears slide along my cheek and drip down into Boo's gray fur. She didn't feel it, and I chose to pretend it wasn't there. The doorbell and knocking made me groan. I knew who it was, and I didn't have the defenses to face him, so I rolled over and faced away from the door, praying he would think no one was home and leave.

Boo jumped down and went to eat in the bathroom, and after a few minutes, the bed dipped, and I rolled over, thinking it was her. Instead, my fist automatically came up, and Antonio caught it before it reached his nose.

"What the hell? How did you get in here?"

"Why are you crying?" He ignored my questions for one of his own.

"I'm not." I sniffed.

"Liar."

He reached up and wiped my tears from my cheek, and stared into my eyes. All at once, the memory of us in the closet at Zucca's flashed through my mind and I remembered I was only wearing a towel.

"Umm." I didn't get to finish. The front door banged open, and Cassy yelled from downstairs. She was quickly followed by the pitter-patter of little feet. "Shit. Cassy's home with Sammie and the twins."

"Go get dressed."

He bounded off the bed and out the door while I went to the closet. I heard the door close while I reached for clothes to put on. Why did I all of a sudden feel like a teenager whose parents just got home? I didn't know what his plan was. I'd never had a situation like this before.

I dressed as quickly as I could and pulled a comb through my curls. No time for a full work-up right now. I'd deal with the frizz later when I'd end up cursing the humidity. With one hand tucking my hair behind my ear, I yanked the door to the hallway open, and there was Cassy between Antonio and the stairs with her arms crossed over her chest, staring him down.

"What's going on?" I asked.

"Tha's what I wanna know. Why you here, Desio?"

"Cassy, what's wrong with you? He's always here."

"Uh-huh, but not in the house whichu alone." She reached out to touch his hair, and he jerked his head back. "How come he got dry hair, and yours is wet?"

"Because I took a shower and nodded off with Boo. I left the front door unlocked by mistake, and Antonio came to check on me. He came in and has been waiting here on the landing for me. Who are you? My mother?"

"Why you been cryin'?" she asked.

I threw up my hands in exasperation. "Because this has been a day from hell, and it's not over yet. I allowed myself a moment of self-pity. Sue me. Now, are we done here? Antonio, I'm sure you have places to be."

"Why isn't your day done yet?" he asked.

"It's this investigation from your—from Wesley. I have to speak to the Investigating Officer tonight and my stomach is in knots. He's going to ask all sorts of questions and rake me over the coals, in the hopes he can either A, get me to contradict myself and make his job easier; B, analyze everything I say to see where he can catch me; or C. Well, I don't have a C. I do need to call Colonel Waters, though, now that I think about it. Excuse me."

I stepped around the two of them, and Antonio turned and followed me down the steps. On the landing outside the kitchen, Ana lifted her arms and I picked her up. I planted a big kiss on her cheek with a loud pop and she giggled.

Sammie turned around in the kitchen and her eyes followed Antonio when he strode around me to the front of the house. I put Ana down and trailed behind him to the door, where I opened it and stepped outside with him.

"She's not my anything, Laci. Why do you keep assigning her importance in my life when there is none?"

"I don't know. It appears you see her more than you do me, and it's unsettling. I don't know why it's bothering me so much; it just is."

"I spend more with her, but it's not by choice. The damn woman won't leave me alone. She's tracked my every move and shows up without my knowing it. How the hell does she do that?"

"Aren't you the big shot detective? I figured you'd have her figured out already. Did she put something on your car? Wait. Where is your car?"

"I left it around the corner in case you didn't want to see me," he said. I took off down the sidewalk and was halfway to the street leading to the rowhouse behind mine when he caught up. He spoke to my back because I was on a mission. "Where are you going?"

"To help you look over your car for a device," I said. "If indeed it is here." At the end of the row of houses, I looked and there was no car. "Okay, I give. Where's your car?"

"Laci!" Cassy yelled from the front of our house.

"What?" I yelled back.

"Someone got to Dan Bishop. He done been poisoned." I met Cassy halfway to the house. Antonio trailed behind me.

"What? But that's impossible. Mrs. Zimmer is in the hospital, and Haylee and Ted are in jail. Who else is left?" I slapped myself on the forehead. "It's Mr. Zimmer. The husband. Quick, Desio, call Deputy Robinson. We need someone with his wife. Now. Make sure there's a guard outside Ruby's room, too."

"How you know it's her husband?" Cassy asked.

"Sammie. She's more intuitive than any of us realize. She mentioned how he looked scared the other day when I questioned him. I thought he was scared for his wife, but no, he's scared for himself."

Once in the house, Cassy and I grabbed our stuff and raced for her car at the curb. Desio decided he would leave it to us and would catch up later to find how everything turned out. We yelled to Sammie on our way out that we didn't know how long we would be. I just hope we were in time to prevent him killing his wife.

"Time like these, I wish I was still a cop and could skip traffic," Cassy said.

"I know," I said. "Colonel Martin isn't answering her phone, so we'll go it alone. Deputy Robinson is going to meet us at the hospital. He's got the sirens we don't."

Less than ten minutes later, we pulled into a spot at the hospital and ran for the front entrance. We bypassed the information desk and ran right on through to Mrs. Zimmer's room. We passed Dr. Tangen on the way, who was running in the same direction we were. I didn't know where he was going, but I knew what room I needed.

Cassy shoved the door to the room open but stopped right inside the door. I stepped from behind her in time to see Deputy Robinson slapping the cuffs on Mr. Zimmer, where he lay sprawled on the floor. Mrs. Zimmer was flat on her back, and nurses were everywhere. Dr. Tangen pushed me out of the way and approached her on the bed.

"How many minutes?" he asked.

"Eight," the nurse replied.

"Keep going. I'll be right back."

We could only stand to the side while Deputy Robinson took Mr. Zimmer away. I didn't know whether to stay with Mrs. Zimmer or follow him. I quickly chose to follow him and dragged Cassy out with me. There was nothing we could do to help her, but we could help Robinson get her husband.

****

Knowing it would take a while to get Mr. Zimmer processed in Bel Air, we took our time getting to him. We stopped at Groov's in Joppatowne, but all I could get down was sweet tea.

"Why you think he did it?" Cassy asked.

"Honestly?" I asked. "I have no idea. We're just going to have to wait for him to tell us. Did he kill Jill?

How is she tied into it? We can't forget that's how we got started in all this."

"True dat," Cassy said. "This thing is full of twists and turns I didn' see comin'."

We picked up our drinks and got in Cassy's car for the drive to the detention center. She didn't crank up her music, which was helpful. This way, I could sort through the information in my head. Sometimes, it was like index cards, and others, such as this, it was like switching commercials before they finished.

Deputy Robinson met us at the door to the detention center and we followed him to the room we met in the last time.

"Has he said anything?" I asked.

"Not really, but then his lawyer just got here."

"Who is this one?" I asked.

"I've never met her before. I hear she's good, though. Her name is Lucretia Edwards."

Cassy sucked in her breath next to me, and I turned toward her. "You know her?"

"I know of her, yeah. She gotta reputation for bein' cutthroat. Ain' nothing she won' do. She' been tryin' to join the DA's office in Baltimore for a couple years."

We sat there another ten minutes when the door opened, and Colonel Martin entered. I immediately stood.

"Colonel, I'm glad you could join us," I said.

I spent the next few minutes catching her up on what brought us here, and when the door opened again, we were all set. Mr. Zimmer entered first with his head down, and Cassy closed the door to the room on her way out. His presence still radiated punctured tea bag, but now there was a bite to it. With him was a petite blonde woman in a power suit. Yeah, she was one not to be messed with. I could tell that already.

"Mr. Zimmer," I said. "Perhaps you could start with what Jill Westfall has to do with all of this? That's where it all began, didn't it?"

"My wife did everything she could for that woman, but it wasn't enough. She wanted more. She wanted Betsey's soul. In exchange for what, you ask? Betsey knew something about Jill, and when Jill showed her true colors in the spouse club thing, Betsey let her know she would need to buy her silence."

"Your wife tried to blackmail Jill?" I asked. "About what?"

"Jill bought drugs from Teddy. That's the reason she was in the hospital. That's how she lost the baby. Wasn't any need for an abortion when she knew where to get drugs to take care of it herself. Ted told Bestey one night after he saw Jill in the neighborhood. He didn't know she lived next door to us. It was just gossip to him, but Betsey used it against her."

"How then did Jill turn it around?" I asked.

"Once Betsey presented her case to Jill and asked for a favor with the club, she began to get the notion she could get some other things. Jill was accommodating at first, but when Betsey asked for something for Ruby, Jill refused. Betsey may have leaned on her a little much after that, but then Jill turned the tables and blackmailed Betsey for blackmailing her."

Only in my wildest imaginings did this make any sense.

"Betsey couldn't believe it. She knew we would be thrown out of our house if word got out. She begged and pleaded, but Jill already made an appointment with General Fields. The clock was ticking, and the noose was tightening on my Betsey."

"How did she kill Jill?" I asked, but he clammed up on me. "Okay, then tell me what happened with Ruby? How did she wind up with an overdose?"

"Betsey gave her the wrong pills," he said.

"Wrong pills?" I asked. "Were they Betsey's? Haylee told us your wife pressured Ruby to take anxiety meds. Why was she adamant that Ruby take her meds? Was she pinning this on Jill? She was going to accuse Jill of planting them there, wasn't she?"

"That's speculation," Lucretia said. She had a deep, sultry voice, and I was surprised by it.

"It isn't speculation if Mr. Zimmer tells us. He's on the hook for the murder of Jill, attempted murder of Ruby, and possible murder of his wife; we don't know her condition yet. Not to mention Dan Bishop. He's the latest to be drugged. All of this stems from your wife and her trying to blackmail Jill for some favors. She met her match with Jill, though. She could give as good as she got, and she pushed back. Mrs. Zimmer got scared and killed Jill, and in covering for your wife, you drugged Ruby to make it look like Jill did it before she died. With Jill gone, no one could prove it and you thought you were home free.

"Then you drugged your wife to make it look like Haylee or Ted. You kept passing the buck like a game of hot potato. Never once did you imagine that you would be the one left holding the spud. I bet that's why you drugged Dan—to make it look like suicide. With him out of the way, you could blame things on Haylee. The one last card in your deck. The nice girl who lived next door and did everything to help you and your wife. This is how you repaid her."

Lucretia was slapping her hand on the table and yelling at me before I finished, but I just got louder and louder. I knew I was right. I knew it as I was sitting there.

"You can't prove any of this, Ms. Duvall," Lucretia said.

"I think your nephew will have a few things to tell us. Won't he, Mr. Zimmer?" I said.

"He won't tell," Mr. Zimmer said.

"If it gets him off the hook for murder and attempted murder, I think he'll have plenty to say," I said. "And it's Special Agent Major Laci Duvall, Air Force OSI, Ms. Edwards." Lucretia suddenly looked sick. Her face went white. I didn't know what that was about, I honestly didn't care. "Deputy Robinson, Mr. Zimmer here is under arrest for the attempted murder of Ruby Moffat, Betsey Zimmer, and Dan Bishop."

Beethoven going off in my purse brought me crashing down to earth. It was the Investigating Officer. I ran from the room so I could take the call. With the door closing behind me, I saw Mr. Zimmer bounce off the table before he crashed into his chair. Lucretia missed it because her attention was focused on me.

Chapter Twenty-Two

"So, he did it?" Cassy asked.

We were at a local pizza place in the city recapping everything for Rev, Antonio, Amaré, and Sammie, who missed the dramatic conclusion.

"He eventually caved when he realized Ted was going to spill on him," I said. "By then, we didn't need Ted's testimony, but it helped since Mrs. Zimmer died in the hospital because of him. He's going away for a long time. As is Ted for being a dealer. Zucca got his bartender back drug-free or in the process of it. Adam's going to rehab with the support of Zucca. He'll be better because of it."

"I can' believe that quiet man did all this," Cassy said.

"I owe it all to Sammie here," I said.

"Me? Why me?" she asked.

"You were the most observant of all of us. In the hospital that day, you mentioned in passing that he was afraid. He was—he didn't want to get caught. I think our visit pushed him into drugging Dan. He was desperate, and the last loose end was his wife."

"Can Mrs. Zimmer be placed at the softball match?" Rev asked.

"Yes, I went back and reviewed the footage we got from Mrs. Bowry. It's plain as day that she parked in one of the spots for Edgewood Neighbor Space and walked across the parking area to the softball game. She was carrying a large straw bag that we're assuming she carried the flamingo and gun in. Deputy Robinson is looking for the gun—he has a warrant to search everything she and her husband own."

"What happened to the spouse's club?" Cassy asked.

"Oh, they disbanded for good," I said. "There will no longer be a spouse's club on post. Ruby and Damian have been granted their request to leave. They'll be moving to New York for Damian to teach at the Academy."

"Is Dan okay?" Sammie asked.

"He is. He and Haylee will be staying here until their assignment is up. Noah, however, has decided to retire and get out of the military altogether." It's probably for the best, knowing what I did about his record. The final nail in the coffin was his wife being murdered. It leaves the question, though—did Jill *and* Noah both get their drugs from Ted? How did they not know the other one was getting drugs? There were still unanswered questions.

The door to the pizza shop opened, and a petite blonde in a power suit walked in with another woman. They went to a booth across the room. I recognized Lucretia when she turned to sit down with her friend. Since I had put her client behind bars, her stony look wasn't lost on me.

"Uh-oh," Amaré said. He glanced at the women and turned back to our table before asking Desio, "Isn't that Lucretia?"

"Yes, tha—" I said.

"I don't think so." Desio interrupted me. "Though

it's been so long, I don't remember."

"It wasn't that long ago, maybe a month or—" Amaré stopped.

It was like a football game—red flags flying all over the place. "Umm, Antonio, how do you know Lucretia Edwards?"

"You want to see the game room, Cassy?" Amaré asked. "They got an arcade."

"Oh hell, no. I wanna hear what the detective here has to say," Cassy said.

"Cass," Amaré said with a touch of warning.

"Fine—show me the damn arcade. Laci'll tell me later anyways. Wonchu?" she asked.

I grinned as Sammie and Rev hopped up to join Cassy and Amaré. I probably shouldn't be enjoying Desio's discomfort this much, but I so seldom got to see it. He recently helped me find my ex-husband's killer. The ex I dumped him for. You couldn't get much more awkward than that.

"Antonio, it's fine."

He looked at me and then over at the blonde woman at the other table. They had resumed scanning their menus and weren't staring at us anymore. I said that, but when I glanced over again, Lucretia was watching us with her heart in her eyes.

"I dated Lucretia, the blonde woman, for a brief period up until seeing you last month. I may have forgotten to tell her she and I weren't dating anymore. I haven't seen her since our last date the weekend before I saw you in Dr. Mann's office."

"Well, now I know why she hated the sound of my name earlier. How long is a brief period?"

"What? I think our first date was in January," he

said. "It was after the first snow we had."

"Desio, six months is not a brief period. She may have thought you were going somewhere."

"I never said as much." He looked disgruntled and adorable at the same time—for someone carrying a concealed weapon. I glanced over and the friend was heading for the restroom.

"Now's your chance to set the record straight, Antonio," I said. "Go talk to her."

He let out a long sigh. "You're not going to let this go, are you?"

When I shook my head, he got out of the seat and went to her table. She looked up as he got closer and broke into a big smile, but the smile faded the longer he talked, and she anxiously fiddled with her ponytail. She nodded her head in answer to his question, and then he turned back toward me. I watched her while he approached our table, and she looked ready to break into tears.

"Didn't it go well?" I asked.

"What? Oh, it was fine."

"Then why so sad?" I asked.

"I may have ended a possible relationship for no reason."

I knew what he was saying. "Antonio." I reached and took his hand in mine. "I'm not going anywhere. I promise you I won't make that mistake again."

Our food arrived just as the gang joined us again. We kept the conversation light while we ate, but I noticed when the friend came back, the two women left the restaurant without ordering anything.

I wondered how many dates they had gone on. If our history was any comparison, it wasn't many at all.

We were currently sitting at zero.

"You didn' tell us what happened with Wesley," Cassy said, "and the investigation."

"The investigation is over. I've been cleared." I let my breath out on a long exhale. So long I got dizzy and grabbed my sweet tea and took a swig.

"It's really over?" Sammie asked.

"Yep. Wesley's been relocated, and a new member of the team is on their way here."

"Wait, she's gone?" Rev asked.

"Yep. Turns out she wasn't pregnant after all, and there was no husband. Which is why she's now on her way to Walter Reed, where she'll undergo a mental evaluation before they decide what to do with her."

"Holy cow," Sammie whispered.

"No kidding," I said.

A word about the author…

Pamela Kyel was born and raised in Edgewood, Maryland—north of Charm City. It's a running joke when you live near a large, well-known city—you tell people that's where you're from. So, unofficially, she's from Baltimore! Since her spouse's retirement from the military, they call Wisconsin home, where they have two daughters and two cats, Daisy and Ernie. You can follow along with her on her website, www.pamelakyel.com.